it could happen!

in an adult playground...

"She was lovely. Long perfect legs, deep-red hair worn longer than shoulder length, the face of an arrogant angel and a body so perfect it seemed unreal. Her only garment was a cloak of glowing blue velvet."

—*cloak of anarchy* by larry niven

money to buy the past...

"This was not going to be just another Howard Johnson gas-station sale; even something like an old Hilton or the Cooperstown Baseball Hall of Fame I unloaded last year was thinking too small. In his own way Ito was telling me that price was no object; the sky was the limit. This was the dream of a lifetime! A sucker with a bottomless bank account placing himself trustingly in my tender hands!"

—*a thing of beauty* by norman spinrad

2020 vision

Also edited
by Jerry Pournelle:

BLACK HOLES   23962 $1.95

Buy them at your local bookstore or use this handy coupon for ordering.

This offer expires 2/28/81   8999

2020 vision

edited by

jerry pournelle

fawcett crest ● new york

For John McCarthy, who builds futures

2020 VISION

Published by Fawcett Crest Books, a unit of CBS Publications, the
Consumer Publishing Division of CBS Inc.

Copyright © 1974, 1980 by Jerry Pournelle
ALL RIGHTS RESERVED

ISBN: 0-449-24302-8

The stories in this work were previously published in 1974 by Avon
Books.

The Preface, Introduction, Afterword, and editorial comments have
not previously been published.

Because the individual story copyright information would not fit on
this page, the following acknowledgments should be considered an
extension of the copyright page.

Printed in the United States of America

First Fawcett Crest printing: June 1980

10 9 8 7 6 5 4 3 2 1

acknowledgments

contents

preface

Can science-fiction writers predict the future? More important, can they do it entertainingly?

The second question is the more *important. A reader who wants straight technological forecasting or socio-economic projection can turn to the professional futurists such as Herman Kahn and to organizations such as the World Future Society. There are lots of outfits whose job it is to foretell the future; some do it well, some very badly. None are all that good at it. Anyone who can* actually *foretell the future doesn't need to write for a living.*

But to answer the second question, yes, of course we can make our forecasts entertaining. That's our business. Science-fiction writers (most SF authors despise the terminally cute abbreviation "Sci-Fi") are bards, and our job isn't all that different from that of the bards of ancient times who sang for their suppers; if we can't entertain, we'll soon be out of a job. Moreover, when I commissioned the stories for this book I made certain I didn't invite anyone who wasn't an entertaining writer.

There remains the first question: Can SF authors predict the future?

That turns out to be a complex question, and there

is no short answer. For those particularly interested I recommend my lengthy essay in the 1981 Britannica Yearbook Science and the Future; *I can only touch on the subject here.*

It is, of course, old-hat to list the astounding predictions of science-fictioneers: the famous 1944 "atom bomb" story by Cleve Cartmill that brought the FBI to the editorial offices of Astounding; *much of the work of H. G. Wells and Jules Verne; Kipling's "With the Night Mail"; there are dozens of good examples. Nuclear power plants, space travel and rocket ships, "beam" weapons; or, going farther back, airplanes and telephones and television—all were, in point of fact, "predicted" by some science-fiction writer in some story or another. There's no point in beating this into the ground; we've trumpeted our successes loudly enough.*

What we don't do is boast of the unsuccessful predictions: the things we forecast that just didn't happen. I leave out "wild talents"—psionic machines and other techniques for using extrasensory perception—because some of that may yet happen. I also leave out faster-than-light travel, because although today's science says that's impossible, I, at least, am not so certain. But ignoring those traditional themes still leaves us thousands of science-fiction ideas that haven't happened and aren't going to happen.

Perhaps more important, neither science-fiction writers nor anyone else forecast certain important developments such as the energy crisis and cheap but very powerful computers. . . .

Some of us did better than others. I take a certain bitter pride in having published in 1971 an article entitled "America's Looming Energy Crisis," and in 1972 a series of short science-fiction stories with titles such

as *"Ecology Now!"* and *"Power to the People"* which
dealt with energy shortages; while Herman Kahn's
Things To Come, *a 1972 professional study of the future,
has not a single index reference to "energy," "oil," "coal,"
or "nuclear power."*

So. We've often been wrong. But so have the profes-
sionals. More to the point, science-fiction writers haven't
always been trying to predict the future. Sometimes
we're only having a bit of fun, or speculating about
"what-if," or trying to make a buck singing for our suppers. Accurate forecasting isn't our real job, and of
course few of us can or would want to employ high-speed
computers, operations research, stochastic modeling,
and the myriad other tools available to the professional
futurists.

But sometimes we do try, and that brings us to this
book.

2020 Vision *is a book of predictions. It was designed
that way. It isn't really a test of SF's power to predict,
because it's primarily meant to entertain, but the ground
rules were simple enough: The authors were asked to
write a story which really and truly might happen in
the year 2020. There were to be no benevolent social
scientists from Alpha Centauri who come to Earth and
solve all our problems—unless, of course, the author
really thinks the Alpha Centaurians are coming in the
next forty years, and that they'll give a damn about
saving us when they get here.*

The stories were written in 1972. You'd think that
dates the book; today we have a whole new set of problems few of us foresaw (recall Herman Kahn's **Things
To Come**) eight years ago—but in fact the stories don't
seem dated at all. These may not be precisely the predictions our authors would make were they given the

same ground rules today, but there's nothing in here that events have made impossible. Some of the stories have held up very well indeed as predictors.

And they always were entertaining.

Jerry Pournelle
Hollywood, 1980

the year 2020

jerry pournelle

Anyone can predict the future—but no one can know he has made an accurate forecast. There are just too many variables. At best one predicts a future: one of many possible scenarios, one of the many ways things may go.

Such scenarios are sometimes known as "futuribles," a portmanteau word made up by Bertrand de Jouvenal for "future" and "possible"; and they can be extremely valuable. Consider: If we are predicting the outcome of tossing a coin, we know what must happen. There are only a few alternatives. Thus one has made no particularly valuable contribution by saying, "Well, a possible future is that the coin will fall heads...."

But when you move to more complex events, such as the future history of mankind, futuribles can be valuable indeed. One obvious use is as blueprints: a good scenario showing a plausible means for overcoming the energy crisis, avoiding the limits to growth, and bringing nearly limitless wealth to all would be no small thing.

Futuribles can also serve as warnings of paths to avoid. Many science-fiction writers have specialized in such jeremiads; two of the best-known SF works of all, Orwell's 1984 and Huxley's Brave New World, are particularly fine examples.

Predictions of future events—whether by science-fiction writers or "professional" futurists—should thus be understood in context: not forecasts of "the" future, but scenarios of possible futures; as "futuribles." This essay is no exception.

the world as it could be made

I recently presented a paper to a session called "The Limits to Knowledge" at an annual meeting of the American Association for the Advancement of Science. Those familiar with my works will not be surprised to find my paper was entitled "The Only Limit Is Nerve." In my judgment there are damned few limits to growth, and none at all for the foreseeable future.

I've presented the view before, most notably in my book of essays A Step Farther Out *(Ace). If we consider the usually forecast dooms—war, famine, pollution, depletion of nonrenewable resources, lack of living space— all but the first are not primary problems. Given sufficient energy, we can feed a hundred times as many people as inhabit Earth at present. Given sufficient energy, there is no pollution: At worst, one can take the pollutants apart into their constituent elements. Given sufficient wealth—and for wealth read cheap energy— we can build "microcities," single structures a square mile or so on a side, containing living space and working place for as many as half a million people; a thousand such could contain the entire population of North America, occupy less space than the city of Los Angeles (although they would of course be scattered about, not piled in one place) and provide much better living conditions than most New Yorkers enjoy. And lack of resources need not concern us, for, although at the moment*

*we live on "Only One Earth," the fact is that we live in
a system of nine planets, thirty eight moons, a million
asteroids, and a billion comets. We've only to go after
them.*

*Nor need we be concerned about energy resources. We
know how to get more than we need.*

*Consider Solar Power Satellites, the ultimate in solar
power. SPS is very expensive; the program would cost
about 100 billion dollars before it delivered a single
kilowatt of power. But once that investment is made,
additional SPS are cheap compared to present power
systems; they never need fuel; and we can build as many
as we want or need. The Sun puts forth limitless power,
more than we ever could need, and it's Out There for
the taking. A fallout benefit of SPS is that we would
have to construct space factories and moon mines as part
of the building process; we'd have those as a bonus. We
could do science on weekends; and we'd provide a new
cutting edge to our technological advancement.*

*Of course SPS may not be the best way to go; my
point is that we need not stop the show for lack of energy.
Progress need not end. We have at least one pathway to
a limitless future. In the words of Peter Vajk's new book,*
Doomsday Has Been Cancelled.

*The future we could build is presented in great and
fascinating detail by Robert Prehoda in a new work
entitled* Your Next Fifty Years *(Ace), and in a number
of others I recommend, including Adrian Berry's* The
Next Ten Thousand Years *(Dutton), and Harry Stine's*
The Third Industrial Revolution *(Ace); as well as in
my own* A Step Farther Out. *I've no room to go into
great detail here. The point is that we need not fear the
future. There are limitless possibilities within our grasp.
We could by 2020 build a world in which the Earth is
a park, and all the messy and polluting activities of*

*civilization are carried out in space; a world of Moon
and asteroid mines, undersea cities, the whole panoply
of what is usually called "that Buck Rogers stuff." It
doesn't have to be science fiction. We really and truly
can do it.*

But will we?

*Solving the energy crisis will take money and lots of
it. Not a lot compared even to a medium-sized war, not
much compared to a great Depression, but still a lot. We
have the money; we spend more every year on liquor, or
on cigarettes, or on cosmetics than is needed to build
that dream world of limitless possibilities. We need only
get at it.*

*Even as I write this, technology marches on. It is
interesting to note that every year the life expectancy of
a man my age increases by one year; if that trend continues, most of those who read this book will be alive
and active in the year 2020. I am writing this on a
computer named Ezekial—my own computer, paid for,
which sits here in my office and which gives me more
computing power than the United States government
could buy for a billion dollars in 1965. It is already
obsolete; for less than I paid for Ezekial I could buy a
considerably more powerful machine. (No, no, Zeke, I
am not contemplating replacing you!)*

*By 2020 we could have information nets that would
let anyone get the answer to literally any question the
answer to which is known or calculable. Every book ever
written; every table of data; complex equations and for-
mulae; all instantly available on a home computer connected by telephone to a large central data bank. None
of that requires any new technology. We could build
such "information utilities" now with existing equipment, for not much more than one thousand dollars per
household—and those costs will plummet if we start*

building home computers by the million. By 2020 computers will be built into every television set, i.e., be essentially free.

Consider that the year 2020 is no further from us than the year 1940; contemplate what's happened since 1940; and recall that technology is accelerating, change becomes more rapid each year; and you will understand that most forecasts, including those of science-fiction writers, are far too conservative.

Since 1940 we have built the Interstate Highway grid. For a lot less than that we could have factories in space and on the Moon. Between 1942 and 1945 we sent more than two million soldiers to Europe and the Far East—and brought them home again. For a lot less than that cost we could send hundreds of thousands to the asteroid belt. In the past ten years we have sent probes to Mars, Jupiter, and Saturn; within the next ten we could orbit a telescope that would daily give us better pictures of those planets than the probes delivered, a telescope able not only to see planets (if there are any) circling the nearer stars such as Alpha Centauri, but also to study their cloud structure.

In 1940 the fastest planes in existence could go 350 miles an hour, and the DC-3 "gooney bird" was an advanced ship. In 1940 radio was an entertaining but not too reliable mass medium, and there was no television. In 1940 the "miracle drug" was sulfa, and there were no antibiotics. Half the population worked on farms, and farm production was a fraction of today's yields. There were no computers at all; the Norden bombsight and navy mechanical-analogue fire-control systems were the most advanced computing devices known. A good part of the country didn't have electricity (I lived on a farm eight miles outside Memphis and we had kerosene lamps for our light at night). There were almost no plastics—no styrofoam iceboxes and cups, no Melmac dinner plates, no acrylic false teeth. No pacemakers; no electroencephalographs; few electrocardiograph machines; most of the tools and drugs modern physicians consider indispensable either did not exist or were to be found only in the most advanced (and expensive) clinics and hospitals.

And technology is accelerating. The year 2020 can, if things continue as they are at present, be as far advanced over 1980 as 1980 is over, not 1940, but 1920.

Of course there will be problems. Technology presents opportunities to harm as well as help. But our problems of forty years from now need not be problems of scarcity.

We've only to decide to build that future. We know how to do it.

the grim world that may be

There is another possibility. Life in the year 2020 could be grim indeed, and our descendents may look back on 1980 as a Golden Age. Unfortunately it's very easy to see disastrous futuribles.

The most obvious is war. As early as 1936 Stephen Vincent Benet could ask:

Where are you coming from, soldier, grim soldier,
    with weapons beyond the reach of my mind...

and receive for answer:

Stand out of my way and be silent before me,
    for none shall come after me, foeman or friend...

Albert Jay Nock, also writing in the thirties, believed we were slowly passing into a new Dark Age; a theme chillingly echoed and convincingly presented by Roberto Vacca in this decade.

Dr. Isaac Asimov has a whole list of reasons why we're all doomed. They can be summed up in his famous vision of the future: Crowded! *Many professional futurists (with the notable exception of Herman Kahn) share that view. One issue of* The Futurist *put it thusly: "Man appears to be heading toward a calamitous Day of Reckoning. Unless his rapidly growing population and expanding industrial capacity is somehow brought under control, the Earth's natural resources will be exhausted and the environment so polluted that the world will no longer be livable."*

During the 1970's the most influential book on university campuses across the nation was The Limits to Growth, *followed closely by* Small is Beautiful; *both argued for Zero Growth in both population and industry as the* only *road to survival.*

If we adopt the Zero Growth philosophy, we will almost certainly think of 1980 as a Golden Age.

Consider: With the most stringent regulation, we are unlikely to stop population growth for decades. Oh, sure, in the West we already have population stability: Were it not for immigration, the U.S. would actually have a slightly declining population. But in most of the world there's nothing like stabilization, and won't be for a while. But we can stop industrial growth pretty rapidly (in fact we darned near have stopped it; as I write this, I see in the Wall Street Journal *that U.S. productivity and production declined in calendar 1979). The goodies available for distribution remain constant or decline in a ZG world; but the number of people wanting a share of the pie continues to grow. . . .*

At best, then, 2020 under ZG would be a world in which the West is an island of relative wealth in the middle of a vast sea of eternal poverty and misery. The psychological effect of that isn't easily predicted: Might we try to "justify" our hogging most of the wealth, and thus end up with elitist theories? Fascism? It certainly seems possible.

Meanwhile, we really are running low on energy; and so far all of Washington's "remedies" have been ways to equalize misery rather than solve the problem. Rationing, new taxes, regulations, have been proposed, but no massive research efforts.

Recall that the President spoke for an hour on the energy crisis and did not once mention the words "research" or "technology"; and that of over a hundred people whose advice was sought at the famous Camp David "energy retreat," not one was a scientist or engineer. We're closing down nuclear plants; we have no timetable for developing fusion; we've scrapped plans for building fast-breeder reactors; and we've just about scrubbed the space program. There's some money for windmills and ground-based solar-power systems, but no serious analyst of America's energy needs believes that either is more than a stunt. The Department of Energy has already determined that there isn't enough wind even if the mills were cheap—and they're not; while ground-based solar requires hundreds of square miles of collectors and suffers from fatal defects not shared by space-based solar systems: on Earth the Sun doesn't shine much at night or when it's raining. Proper research might solve the energy problem, but sharing misery doesn't help much.

We really might spiral down into the muck. Increasing energy costs bring on crippling inflation, productivity drops again, we fall into a new Great Depression;

existing power plants wear out and are not replaced; the space shuttle is delayed again and again until it is finally abandoned . . .

That scenario leads to a 2020 in which 1980 looks like a Golden Age indeed.

where to from here?

"The future is a race between utopia and oblivion."

—R. Buckminster Fuller

Fuller sums it nicely: There doesn't seem a lot of intermediate choice. We can build toward a new utopia, a society of immense capabilities and wealth—or we can spiral back into the muck.

Fortunately the time to choose has not passed. For yet a little while we can hang on, continue much as we have for the past decades, and still retain the capability for building utopia.

I do not think we can put off the decision for many decades more. It is possible that the 1980's will be the crucial period; it seems certain that by the year 2000 we will irrevocably have chosen. If by then we have not made the decision to invest in the future, and committed massive resources into building a bright new future, we may not have the resources to commit.

Item: The average age of the U.S. population is rising. It will continue to creep up, leaving proportionately fewer people in the work force. Our social security system is of course not an insurance system at all; it is based on the assumption of constantly rising production, a

scheme to tax the present work force to support the re-
tired. The system is bankrupt. So are most other pension
and retirement funds. It is estimated that by the year
2020 the retirement-pay obligations of the city of Los
Angeles will be twice the entire 1980 budget. Thus, they
are not going to be paid. . . .

In other words, we must increase the productivity per
worker, or we will all experience a fairly precipitous
drop in standard of living. And that's here in the U.S.

Meanwhile, at present rates of capital formation there
is not the ghost of a chance that the "developing" nations
can build themselves into high-energy societies. Back
in 1970 it took some $30,000 to create a job in the U.S.A.;
multiply that by the projected number of people wanting
jobs in the year 2020 and you get several quadrillions
of dollars—literally more money than there is in the
world, more than the total value of all real and chattel
property on Earth.

Once again we need a quantum jump: great increases
in productivity if the less fortunate nations are to build
themselves even to the point where we were in 1940.

In fact, without some kind of population stability they
can't do it at all. It has been estimated that it requires
a block of farmland the size of the state of Illinois to feed
the annual population increase of India: a new Illinois
every year to stave off famine. Clearly the best technology
can't cope with that.

But assume new birth-control methods. Professor
Jack Cohen of Birmingham University in England is
developing one highly promising method which appears
to be both (1) effective and (2) acceptable to the major
world religions. There will be a lag even so, of course;
but some of the great population spurts in the Eastern
world are due to decreased infant mortality and increased female survival, as the great population spurt

*in the Western world is almost entirely due to the dis-
covery by an Hungarian physician named Ignatz Sammelweis that if doctors and midwives washed their
hands the mothers wouldn't die of the mysterious
childbed fever....(Incidentally, Sammelweis was put
in a madhouse by his fellow physicians, who simply
wouldn't believe him.)*

*Given at least the possibility of population stability,
there are plenty of new technologies.*

*The most spectacular is space, a truly endless frontier.
There is incredible wealth in the solar system. We already know the random rocks on the Moon contain as
high a proportion of useful minerals as some of our best
mine sites on Earth. The Sun pours out energy in vast
quantities, most of it wasted into the black of space; it's
out there, ready to tap, a never-ending river of energy
once we've built space dams....*

*Less spectacularly there is the sea, which also collects
vast amounts of energy in the form of heat.*

*And without new technology at all we still have ways
to transform the developing nations: At Oak Ridge National Laboratories they've developed a whole program
for the instant industrialization of bleak areas like the
Rann of Kutch, the Namib Desert, Sinai, and the coasts
of the Red Sea. The scheme makes use of fast-breeder
fission-power plants (a known U.S.-invented technology; although the U.S. has never built anything larger
than a demonstration plant, the British and French
have a couple in operation, and the Soviet Union has
at least two and is building more.) The plants produce
electricity, which is used to desalinate water. The water
supports crops (literally making the deserts bloom).
More than that, the bitters of leftover sea water, the
concentrated gup left after fresh water is extracted, are
incredibly valuable and can be mined for chemicals and*

minerals. *The waste heat or "thermal pollution" of the system is used to heat the bitterns and speed evaporation, greatly aiding the mining operations. This is all known technology, most right off the shelf. Of course it's expensive. Interestingly enough, the Saudis have both the money and an ideal location....*

Other hopes for cheap energy include fusion, which gets funded in a strange on-again-off-again manner, sometimes getting plenty of money, at other times having to lay off scientists. Fusion, of course, requires new engineering techniques; new science is not required. However, we don't yet know how to build even a proof-of-principle reactor. Incidentally, Robert W. Bussard, inventor of the Bussard ramjet, beloved of certain science-fiction writers, has developed what he calls a "throwaway" small fusion reactor which looks in theory to be constructible. There's been a lot of acrimonious debate about why the Department of Energy refused funding to build one; one theory is that they're afraid it might work. After all, if you have a good energy source, you no longer need a Department of Energy (with an annual budget larger than the combined profits of all major oil companies in 1979)....

But we do seem to have the technological resources to save the Golden Age, if we get cracking.

We may not have the will.

When Ben Bova wrote this, he was even as you and I: a working stiff. Since that time, of course, he has become a giant in the science-fiction community.

John W. Campbell, Jr., was unarguably the most influential single editor in the history of science fiction. He became editor of Astounding Science Fiction *in 1938, and built that pulp magazine into the major publication of the field. By his insistence on plausible science and quality writing, he created the Golden Age of science fiction. Even his detractors give him full credit for his unique influence on the field.*

John died in 1971; and in early 1972 Ben Bova was selected to fill Mr. Campbell's chair. It was no comfortable seat.

Ben continued Campbell's tradition of quality writing and sound scientific background; and he won the Hugo as best editor every year he was eligible. (He became fiction editor, later managing editor, of Omni *magazine in 1978.)*

It's not hard to see why fans voted him awards. Ben came to Analog *(Campbell renamed the magazine in 1960) with hard experience in the real world of science and technology. He was technical editor for Project Vanguard, and later became Manager of Marketing for the Avco Everett Research Laboratory. Bova has seen NASA and the aerospace industry from the inside, and his visions of the future reflect something we all know but hate to admit: Technology may be created by scientists and engineers, but its fate is controlled by politicians.*

However much we'd like to think so, the political decision-makers in 2020 won't be any bigger men than those of 1970; but their problems may be tougher. In Bova's 2020 vision there is still time to make the right decision; but not much time to spare. . . .

build me a mountain

by ben bova

As soon as he stepped through the acoustical screen at the apartment doorway, the noise hit him like a physical force. Chet Kinsman stood there a moment and watched them. *My battlefield,* he thought.

The room was jammed with guests making cocktailparty chatter. It was an old room, big, with a high, ornately paneled ceiling.

He recognized maybe one-tenth of the people. Over at the far end of the room, tall drink in his hand, head slightly bent to catch what some wrinkled matron was saying, stood the target for tonight: Congressman Neal McGrath, swing vote on the House Appropriations Committee.

"Chet, you did come after all!"

He turned to see Mary-Ellen McGrath approaching him, her hand extended in greeting.

"I hardly recognized you without your uniform," she said.

He smiled back at her. "I thought Air Force blue would be a little conspicuous around here."

"Nonsense. And I wanted to see your new oak leaves. A major now."

A captain on the Moon and a major in the Pentagon. Hazardous-duty pay.

"Come on, Chet. I'll show you where the bar is." She took his arm and towed him through the jabbering crowd.

Mary-Ellen was almost as tall as Kinsman. She had the strong, honest face of a woman who can stand beside her husband in the face of anything from Washington cocktail parties to the tight infighting of rural Maine politics.

The bar dispenser hummed absentmindedly to itself as it produced a heavy Scotch and water. Kinsman took a stinging sip of it.

"I was worried you wouldn't come," Mary-Ellen said over the noise of the crowd. "You've been something of a hermit lately."

"Uh-huh."

"And I never expected you to show up by yourself. Chet Kinsman without a girl on his arm is ... well, something new."

"I'm preparing for the priesthood."

"I'd almost believe it," she said straight-faced. "There's something different about you since you've been on the Moon. You're quieter. . . ."

I've been grounded. Aloud, he said, "Creeping maturity. I'm a late achiever."

But she was serious, and as stubborn as her husband. "Don't try to kid around it. You've changed. You're not playing the dashing young astronaut any more."

"Who the hell is?"

A burly, balding man jarred into Kinsman from behind, sloshing half his drink out of its glass.

"Whoops, didn't get it on ya, did ... oh, hell, Mrs. McGrath. Looks like I'm waterin' your rug."

"It's disposable," Mary-Ellen said. "Do you two know each other? Tug Wynne. . . ."

"I've seen Major Kinsman on the Hill."

Chet said, "You're with Allnews Syndicate, aren't you?"

Nodding, Wynne replied, "Surprised to see you here, Major, after this morning's committee session."

Kinsman forced a grin. "I'm an old family friend. Mrs. McGrath and I went to college together."

"You think the congressman's gonna vote against the Moonbase appropriation?"

"Looks that way," Kinsman said.

Mary-Ellen kept silent.

"He sure gave your Colonel Murdock a hard time this morning. Mrs. McGrath, you shoulda seen your husband in action." Wynne chuckled wheezily.

Kinsman changed the subject. "Say, do you know Cy Calder . . . old guy, works for Allied News in California?"

"Only by legend," Wynne answered. "He died a couple months ago, y'know."

"No . . . I didn't know." Kinsman felt a brief pang deep inside the part of him that he kept frozen. He made himself ignore it.

"Yep. He musta been past eighty. Friend of yours?"

"Sort of. I knew him . . . well, a few years back."

Mary-Ellen said, "I'd better get to some of the other guests. There are several old friends of yours here to-night, Chet. Mix around, you'll find them."

With another rasping cackle, Wynne said, "Guess we *could* let somebody else get next to the bar."

Kinsman started to drift away, but Wynne followed beside him.

"Murdock send you over here to try to soften up McGrath?"

Pushing past a pair of arguing cigar smokers, Kinsman frowned. "I was invited to this party weeks ago. I told you, Mrs. McGrath and I are old friends."

"How do you get along with the congressman?"

"What's that supposed to mean?"

Wynne let his teeth show. "Well, from what I hear, you were quite a hell-raiser a few years back. How'd you and Mrs. McGrath get along in college together?"

You cruddy old bastard. "If you're so interested in Mrs. McGrath's college days, why don't you ask her? Or her husband? Get off my back."

Wynne shrugged and raised his glass in mock salute. "Yes sir, Major, sir."

Kinsman turned and started working his way toward the other end of the room. A grandfather clock chimed off in a corner, barely audible over the human noises and clacking of ice in glassware. *Eighteen hundred. Colt and Smitty ought to be halfway to Copernicus by now.*

And then he heard her. He didn't have to see her; he knew it was Diane. The same pure, haunting soprano: a voice straight out of a legend.

Once I had a sweetheart, and now I have none.
Once I had a sweetheart, and now I have none.
He's gone and leave me, he's gone and leave me,
He's gone and leave me to sorrow and mourn.

Her voice stroked his memory and he felt all the old joys, all the old pain, as he pushed his way through the crowd.

Finally he saw her, sitting cross-legged on a sofa, guitar hiding her slim figure. The same ancient guitar: no amplifiers, no boosters. Her hair was still long and straight and black as space; her eyes even darker and deeper. The people were ringed around her, standing, sitting on the floor. They gave her the entire sofa to herself, like an altar that only the anointed could use.

They watched her and listened, entranced by her voice. But she was somewhere else, living the song, seeing what it told of, until she strummed the final chord.

Then she looked straight at Kinsman. Not surprised, not even smiling, just a look that linked them as if the past five years had never been. Before either of them could say or do anything, the others broke into applause. Diane smiled and mouthed "Thank you."

"More, more!"

"Come on, another one."

"'Greensleeves.'"

Diane put the guitar down carefully beside her, uncoiled her long legs, and stood up. "Would later be okay?"

Kinsman grinned. He knew it would be later or nothing.

They muttered reluctant agreement and broke up the circle around her. Kinsman took the final few paces and stood before Diane.

"Good to see you again."

"Hello, Chet." She wasn't quite smiling.

"Here, Diane, I brought you some punch." Kinsman turned to see a fleshy-faced man with a droopy mustache and tousled brown hair, dressed in a violet suit, carrying two plastic cups of punch.

"Thank you, Larry. This is Chet Kinsman. Chet, meet Larry Rose."

"Kinsman?"

"I knew Chet in L.A. a few years back, when I was just getting started. You're still in the Air Force, aren't you, Chet?"

"Affirmative." *Play the role.*

Diane turned back to Larry. "Chet's an astronaut. He's been on the moon."

"Oh. That must be where I heard the name. Weren't

you involved in some sort of a rescue? One of your people got stranded or something and you—"

"Yes." Kinsman cut him short. "It was blown up out of proportion by the news people."

They stood there for a moment, awkwardly silent while the party pulsated around them.

Diane said, "Mary-Ellen told me you might be here tonight. You and Neal are both working on something about the space program?"

"Something like that. Organized any more peace marches?"

She laughed. "Larry, did I ever tell you about the time we tried to get Chet to come out and join one of our demonstrations? In his uniform?"

Larry shook his head.

"Do you remember what you told me, Chet?"

"No. . . . I remember it was during the Brazilian crisis. You were planning to invade the U.C.L.A. library or something. I had flying duty that day."

It was a perfect day for flying, breaking out of the coastal haze and standing the jet on her tailpipe and ripping through the clouds until even the distant Sierras looked like nothing more than wrinkles. Then flat out over the Pacific at mach 5, the only sounds in your earphones from your own breathing and the faint, distant crackle of earthbound men giving orders to other men.

"You told me," Diane said, "that you'd rather be flying patrol and making sure that nobody bombs us while we demonstrated for peace."

She was grinning at him. It was funny now; it hadn't been then.

"Yeah, I guess I did say that."

"How amusing," Larry said. "And what are you

doing now? Protecting us from the Lithuanians? Or going to Mars?"

You overstuffed fruit, you wouldn't even fit into a flight crewman's seat. "I'm serving on a Pentagon assignment. My job is congressional liaison."

"Twisting congressmen's arms is what he means," came Neal McGrath's husky voice from behind him.

Kinsman turned.

"Hello, Chet, Diane . . . eh, Larry Rose, isn't it?"

"You have a good memory for names."

"Goes with the job." Neal McGrath topped Kinsman's six feet by an inch. He was red-haired and rugged-looking. His voice was soft, throaty. Somehow the natural expression of his face, in repose, was an introspective scowl. But he was smiling now. *His cocktail-party smile,* thought Kinsman.

"Tug Wynne tells me I was pretty rough on your boss this morning," McGrath said to Kinsman. The smile turned a shade self-satisfied.

"Colonel Murdock lost a few pounds, and it wasn't all from the TV lights," Kinsman said.

"I was only trying to get him to give me a good reason for funneling money into a permanent Moonbase."

Kinsman answered, "He gave you about fifty reasons, Neal."

"None that hold up," McGrath said. "Not when we've got to find money to reclaim every major city in this country, plus fighting these damned interminable wars."

"And to check the population growth," Diane added.

Here we go again. Shrugging, Kinsman said, "Look, Neal, I'm not going to argue with you. We've been making one-shot missions to the Moon off and on for fifty years now. There's enough there to warrant a permanent base."

McGrath made a sour face. "A big, expensive base on the Moon."

"Makes sense," Kinsman slid in. "It makes sense on a straight cost-effectiveness basis. You've seen the numbers. Moonbase will save you billions of dollars in the long run."

"That's just like Mary-Ellen saves me money at department store sales. I can't afford to save that money. Not this year. The capital outlay is too high. To say nothing of the overruns."

"Now wait...."

"Come on, Chet. There's never been a big program that's lived within its budget. No ... Moonbase is going to have to wait, I'm afraid."

"We've already waited fifty years."

A crowd was gathering around them now, and McGrath automatically raised his voice a notch. "Our first priority has got to be for the cities. They've become jungles, unfit for sane human life. We've got to reclaim them, and save the people who're trapped in them before they all turn into savages."

Damn, he's got a thick hide. "Okay, but it doesn't have to be either/or. We can do both."

"Not while the war's on."

Hold your temper; don't fire at the flag. "The war's an awfully convenient excuse for postponing commitments. We've been in hot and cold wars since before you and I were born."

With the confident grin of a hunter who had cornered his quarry, McGrath asked, "Are you suggesting that we pull our troops out of South America? Or do you want to let our cities collapse completely?"

Do you still beat your wife? "All I'm suggesting,"

Kinsman said with deliberate calm, "is that we shouldn't postpone building Moonbase any longer. We've got the technology—we know how to do it. It's either build a permanent base on the Moon, or stop the lunar exploration program altogether. If we fail to build Moonbase, your budget-cutting friends will throttle down the whole manned space program to zero within a few years."

Still smiling, McGrath said, "I've heard all that from your Colonel Murdock."

There was a curious look in Diane's dark eyes. "Chet . . . why do you want to have a Moonbase built?"

"Why? Because . . . I was just telling you—"

She shook her head. "No, I don't mean the official reasons. I mean why do *you* dig the idea?"

"We need it. The space program needs it."

"No," she said patiently. *"You.* Why are you for it? What's in it for you?"

"What do you mean?" Kinsman asked.

"What makes you tick, man? What turns you on? Is it a Moonbase? What moves you, Chet?"

They were all watching him, the whole crowd, their faces blank or smirking or inquisitive. Floating weightless, standing on nothing and looking at the overpowering beauty of Earth—rich, brilliant, full, shining against the black emptiness. Knowing that people down there are killing each other, teaching their children to kill, your eyes filling with tears at the beauty and sadness of it. How could they see it? How could they understand?

"What moves you, Chet?" Diane asked again.

He made himself grin. "Well, for one thing, the Pentagon-cafeteria coffee."

Everybody laughed. But she wouldn't let him off the hook. "No—get serious. This is important. What turns you on?"

Stall. They don't really want to know. And they wouldn't understand anyway. "You mean aside from the obvious things, like women?"

She nodded gravely.

"Hmmm. I don't know. It's kind of hard to answer. Flying, I guess. Getting out on your own responsibility, away from committees and chains of command."

"There's got to be more to it than that," Diane insisted.

"Well... have you ever been out on the desert at an Israeli outpost, dancing all night by firelight because at dawn there's going to be an attack and you don't want to waste a minute of life?"

There was a heartbeat's span of silence. Then one of the women asked in a near-whisper, "When... were you..."

Kinsman said, "Oh, I've never been there. But isn't it a romantic picture?"

They all broke into laughter. *That burst the bubble.* The crowd began to dissolve, breaking up into smaller groups, dozens of private conversations filling the silence that had briefly held them.

"You cheated," Diane said.

"Maybe I did."

"Don't you have anything except icewater in your veins?"

He shrugged. "If you prick us, do we not bleed?"

"Don't talk dirty."

He took her by the arm and headed for the big glass doors at the far end of the room. "Come on, we've got a lot of catching up to do. I've bought all your tapes."

"And I've been watching your name on the news."

"Don't believe most of it."

He pushed the door open and they stepped out onto the balcony. Shatterproof plastic enclosed the balcony and shielded them from the humid, hazy Washington air—and anything that might be thrown or shot from the street far below. The air conditioning kept the balcony pleasantly cool.

"Sunset," Diane said, looking out toward the slice of sky that was visible between the two apartment buildings across the avenue. "Loveliest time of the day."

"Loneliest time, too."

She turned to him, her eyes showing genuine surprise. "Lonely? You? I didn't know you had any weaknesses like that."

"I've got a few, hidden away here and there."

"Why do you hide them?"

"Because nobody gives a damn about them, one way or the other." Before Diane could reply, he said, "I sound sorry for myself, don't I?"

"Well...."

"Who's this Larry character?"

"He's a very nice guy," she said firmly. "And a good musician. And he doesn't go whizzing off into the wild blue yonder...or space is black, isn't it?"

He nodded. "I don't go whizzing any more, either. I've been grounded."

She blinked at him. "What does that mean?"

"Grounded," Kinsman repeated. "Deballed. No longer qualified for flight duty. No orbital missions. No lunar missions. They won't even let me fly a plane any more. Got some shavetail to jockey me around. I work at a desk."

"But...why?"

"It's a long dirty story. Officially, I'm too valuable to risk or something like that."

"Chet, I'm so sorry...flying meant so much to you, I know." She stepped into his arms and he kissed her.

"Let's get out of here, Diane. Let's go someplace safe and watch the Moon come up and I'll tell you all the legends about your namesake."

"Same old smooth talker."

"No, not any more. I haven't even touched a woman since . . . well, not for a long time."

"I can't leave the party, Chet. They're expecting me to sing."

"Screw them."

"All of them?"

"Don't talk dirty."

She laughed, but shook her head. "Really, Chet. Not now."

"Then let me take you home afterward."

"I'm staying here tonight."

There were several things he wanted to say, but he checked himself.

"Chet, please don't rush me. It's been a long time."

It sure as hell has.

They went back into the party and separated. Kinsman drifted through the crowd, making meaningless chatter with strangers and old friends alike, drink in one hand, occasionally nibbling on a canapé about the size and consistency of spacecraft food. But his mind was replaying, over and over again, the last time he had seen Diane.

Five years ago.

Soaring across the California countryside, riding the updrafts along the hillsides and playing hide-and-seek with the friendly chaste-white cumuli, the only sound the rush of air across the glass bubble an inch over your head, your guts held tight as you sweep and bank and then soar up, up past the clouds and then you bank way over so you're hanging by the shoulder harness and looking straight down into the green citrus groves below.

*Diane sitting in the front seat, so all you can see of her
is the back of her plastic safety helmet. But you can hear
her gasp.*

"Like it?"

"It's wild...gorgeous!"

And then back on the ground. Back in reality.

*"Chet, I've got to go to this meeting. Can't you come
along with me?"*

"No. Got to report for duty."

Just like that. An hour of sharing his world, and
then gone. The last he had seen of her. Until tonight.

The crowd had thinned out considerably. People
were leaving. McGrath was at the hallway door, making the customary noises of farewell. Kinsman spotted
Diane sitting alone on the sofa, tucked against a corner
of it, as if for protection.

He went over and sat down beside her. "I've got news
for you."

"Oh? What?"

"An answer to your question. About what turns me
on. I've been thinking about it all through the party
and I've formed a definite opinion."

She turned to face him, leaning an arm on the sofa's
back. "So what is it?"

"You do. You turn me on."

She didn't look surprised. "Do I?"

Nodding. "Yep. After five years, you still do."

Diane said, "Chet, haven't you learned anything?
We're in two entirely different worlds. You want to go
adventuring."

"And you want to join demonstrations and sing to
the kids about how lousy the world is."

"I'm trying to make the world better!" Her face
looked so damned intent.

"And I'm trying to start a new world."

She shook her head. "We never did see eye to eye on anything."

"Except in bed."

That stopped her, but only for a moment. "That's not enough. Not for me. It wasn't then and it isn't now."

He didn't answer.

"Chet . . . why'd they ground you? What's it all about?"

A hot spark of electricity flashed through his gut. *Careful!* "I told you, it's a long story. I'm a valuable public relations tool for Colonel Murdock. You know, a veteran of lunar exploration. Heroic rescue of an injured teammate. All that crap. So my address is the Pentagon. Level three, ring D, corridor F, room—"

"Whether you like it or not."

"Yes."

"Why don't you quit?"

"And do what? To dig I am not able, to beg I am too proud."

Diane looked at him quizzically. They had both run out of stock answers.

"So there it is," Kinsman said, getting up from the sofa. "Right where we left it five years ago."

Mary-Ellen came over to them. "Don't leave, Chet. We're getting rid of the last of the guests, then we're going to have a little supper. Stay around. Neal wants to talk with you."

"Okay. Fine." *That's what I'm here for.*

"Can I fix you another drink?" Mary-Ellen asked.

"Let me fix you one."

"No, no more for me, thanks."

He looked down at Diane. "Still hooked on *tigres?*"

She smiled. "I haven't had one in years. . . . Yes, I'd like a *tigre.*"

By the time he came back from the bar with the two

smoke-yellow drinks in his hands, the big living room was empty of guests. Diane and Mary-Ellen were sitting on the sofa together. Only when they were this close could you see that they really were sisters. Kinsman heard McGrath out in the hallway, laughingly bidding someone good night.

"Like a family reunion," Kinsman said as he sat on a plush chair facing the sofa.

"You're still here, Chet," McGrath called from the hall archway. "Good. I've got a bone to pick with you, old buddy."

As the congressman crossed to the bar, Mary-Ellen said, "Maybe Diane and I ought to hide out in the kitchen. We can see to supper."

"Not me," Diane said. "I want to be in on this."

Kinsman grinned at her.

McGrath came up and sat beside his wife. The three of them—husband, wife, sister—faced Kinsman. *Like the beginning of a shotgun wedding.*

"Listen, Chet," McGrath began, his voice huskier than usual from too much drinking and smoking. "I don't like the idea of Murdock sending you over here to try to soften me up. Just because you're an old friend doesn't give you—"

"Hold on," Kinsman said. "I was invited here two weeks ago. And I came because I wanted to."

"Murdock knew these hearings were coming up this week and next. Don't deny it."

"I'm not denying a damned thing. Murdock can do what he wants. I came here because I wanted to. If it fits Murdock's grand scheme, so what?"

McGrath reached into his jacket pocket for a cigaret. "I just don't like having space cadets from the Pentagon spouting Air Force propaganda at my parties. Especially when they're old friends. I don't like it."

"What if the old friend happens to believe that the propaganda is right and you're wrong?"

"Oh, come on now, Chet...."

"Look, Neal, on this Moonbase business, you're wrong. Moonbase is essential, no matter what you think of it."

"It's another boondoggle—"

"The hell it is! We either build Moonbase or we stop exploring the Moon altogether. It's one or the other."

McGrath took a deep, calming drag on his cigaret. Patiently, he said, "There's too much to do here on Earth for me to vote for a nickel on Moonbase. Let alone the billions of dollars...."

"The money is chickenfeed. We spend ten times that amount on new cars each year. A penny tax on cigarets will pay for Moonbase."

McGrath involuntarily glanced at the joint in his hand. Scowling, he answered, "We need all the money we can raise to rebuild the cities. We're going under, the cities are sinking into jungles—"

"Who's spouting the party line now?" Kinsman shot back. "Everybody knows about the poor and the cities. And the population overload. And the whole damned social structure. That's a damned safe hobbyhorse to ride in Congress. What we need is somebody with guts enough to stand up for spending two percent of all that money on the future."

"Are you accusing me—"

"I'm saying you're hiding in the crowd, Neal. I don't disagree with the crowd; they're right about the cities and the poor. But there's a helluva lot more to life than that."

Diane cut in. "Chet, what about Moonbase? What good is it? Who will it help? Will it make jobs for the city kids? Will it build schools?"

He stared at her for a long moment. "No," he said at last. "It won't do any of those things. But it won't prevent them from being done, either."

"Then why should we do it?" Diane asked. "For your entertainment? To earn your Colonel Murdock a promotion or something? Why? What's in it for us?"

Standing on the rim of a giant crater, looking down at the tired terraces of rock worn smooth by five eons of meteoric erosion. The flat pitted plain at the base of the slope. The horizon, sharp and clear, close enough to make you think. And the stars beyond. The silence and the emptiness. The freedom. The peace.

"There's probably nothing in it for you. Maybe for your kids. Maybe for those kids in the cities, I don't know. But there's something in it for me. The only way I'll ever get to the Moon again is to push Moonbase through Congress. Otherwise I'm permanently grounded."

"What?"

Diane said, "You mean Murdock won't let you...."

Kinsman waved them quiet. "Officially, I'm grounded. Officially, there are medical and emotional reasons. That's on the record and there's no way to take it off. Unless there's a permanent base on the Moon, a place where a nonpilot passenger can go, then the only people on the Moon will be flight-rated astronauts. So I need Moonbase; I need it. Myself. For purely personal, selfish reasons."

"Being on the Moon means that much to you?" Diane asked.

Kinsman nodded.

"I don't get it," McGrath said. "What's so damned attractive about the Moon?"

"What was attractive about the great American desert?" Kinsman shot back. "Or the poles? Or the Marianas Deep? How the hell should I know? But a while ago you were all asking what turns me on. This does. Being out there, on your own, away from all the sickness and bullshit of this world—that's what I want. That's what I need."

Mary-Ellen shook her head. "But it's so desolate out there . . . foresaken. . . ."

"Have you been there? Have you watched the Earth rise? Or planted footprints where no man has ever been before? Have you ever been anywhere in your life where you really challenged nature? Where you were really on your own?"

"And you still want to go back?" McGrath had a slight grin on his face.

"Damned right. Sitting around here is like being in jail. . . . Know what they call us at the Pentagon? Luniks. Most of the brass think we're nuts. But they use us, just like Murdock is using me. Maybe we *are* crazy. But I'm going to get back there if I have to build a mountain, starting at my desk, and climb up hand over hand."

"But why, Chet?" Diane asked, suddenly intent. *"Why* is it so important to you? Is it the adventure of it?"

"I told you—it's the freedom. There are no rule books up there; you're on your own. You work with people on the basis of their abilities, not their rank. It's—it's just so completely different up there that I can't really describe it. I know we live in a canned environment, physically. If an air hose splits or a pump malfunctions, you could die in seconds. But in spite of that—maybe *because* of that—you're free emotionally. It's you against the universe, you and your friends, your brothers. There's nothing like it here on Earth."

"Freedom," Diane echoed.

"On the Moon," McGrath said flatly.

Kinsman nodded.

Staring straight at him, Diane said slowly, "What you're saying, Chet, is that a new society can be built on the Moon . . . a society completely different from anything here on Earth."

Kinsman blinked. "Did I say that?"

"Yes, you did."

He shrugged. "Well, if we establish a permanent settlement, I guess we'll have to work out some sort of social structure."

"Would you take the responsibility for setting up that social structure?" Diane asked. "Would you shoulder the job of making certain that all the nonsense of Earth is left behind? Would you do the job *right?*"

For a moment, Kinsman didn't know what to answer. Then he said, "I would try."

"You'd take that responsibility?" Diane asked again.

Nodding. "Damned right."

Mary-Ellen looked totally unconvinced. "But who would be willing to live on the Moon? Who would want to?"

"I would," Diane said.

They all turned to look at her. Mary-Ellen shocked, McGrath curious.

"Would you?" Kinsman asked. "Really?"

Very seriously, she replied, "If you're going to build a new world, how could I stay away?"

Kinsman felt himself relax for the first time all evening. "Well, I'll be damned. . . If you can see it. . . ." He started to laugh.

"What's funny?" McGrath asked.

"I've won a convert, Neal. If Diane can see what it's

all about, then we've got it made. The idea of a Moon-base, of a permanent settlement on the Moon—if it gets across to Diane, then the kids will see it, too."

"There are no kids in Congress."

Kinsman shrugged. "That's okay. Congress'll come around sooner or later. Maybe not this year, maybe not until after Murdock retires. But we'll get it. There's going to be a permanent settlement on the Moon. In time for me to get there."

"Chet," Diane said, "it won't be fun. It's going to be a lot of work."

"I know. But it'll be worth the work."

They sat there, eye to eye, grinning at each other.

McGrath slouched back in the sofa. "I guess I'm simply too old to appreciate all this. I don't see how—"

"Neal," Kinsman said, "someday the history books will devote a chapter to the creation of man's first extraterrestrial society. Your name will be in there as one of the founding fathers. The only question is what year will they put down beside your name?"

"You're a cunning bastard," McGrath mumbled.

"And don't you forget it." Kinsman stood up, stretched, then reached a hand out for Diane. "Come on, lunik, let's take a walk. There's a full Moon out tonight. In a couple years I'll show you what a full Earth looks like."

I have only one disagreement with the arguments in this story: when Diane asks of Moonbase, "Who will it help? Will it make jobs for the city kids? Will it build schools?"

the proper answer, in my judgment, is "Yes."

Perhaps it's time we space enthusiasts stopped apologizing, stopped talking about how little the space program costs, and began telling about the benefits.

They are not always obvious, but they certainly are not small.

Item: the entire field of medical technology. This one I know about. I was there. Back in the early sixties we needed to run some extremely high-stress tests on human subjects; and the flight surgeon wouldn't approve the experiment unless we had a working medical-quality electrocardiograph running in real time so that he could monitor the subject's heart. At that time the only way you could get a medical-quality electrocardiogram was in an electrically screened quiet room with an immobilized subject. So we set out to build circuitry that would get one through a pressure suit and out into an extremely noisy laboratory. Did it, too; and from that has come the whole field of modern medical sensors used in hospitals and ambulances.

Item: All of the large glass-fiber structures, including many standard building-prefabrication techniques, were developed by NASA. Most modern fire-fighting technology was developed as part of the space program. All of the modern microminiature computer stuff, including the computer I'm writing this on, would not exist had not the space program needed it. Most of the sensors we use to detect pollution were developed under NASA contracts, and our very knowledge of the worldwide effects of pollution come from satellite data.

I could give literally thousands of such examples; but perhaps the most important of all is management. APOLLO was an incredibly complex project, with tens of thousands of people working at hundreds of thousands of tasks, some of which we didn't know how to do before we started, and all of which had to be accomplished on time. The human race has no precedent for that; the only thing that comes close is war. Learning how to do vast projects for peaceful ends cannot have harmed our future.

There aren't many millionaire science-fiction writers, and, as far as I know, only one who made his pile the hard way, out of writing income. Larry Niven managed the easy way: He chose the right ancestors. His great-grandfather Doheny discovered oil in the Los Angeles basin.

With old money—and in Los Angeles, fourth generation is old money indeed—Larry doesn't have to write for a living. Fortunately for those of us addicted to his stories, he does it anyway. Some years ago, after I'd been reading his hard-science stories and liked them a lot, I proposed that we collaborate on a book. "Stick with me," I said. "I'll make you rich and famous."

"I'm already rich," quoted Niven.

There was only one answer to that. "Fine," says I. "I'll get rich. You'll get famous."

The result was three novels in print so far, and at least two to come. We've worked together for nearly ten years now.

If you can call it work. That is: I call it work. Like most writers, I love to have written, but I hate to write. I'd have thought Niven was the same way, but no; for him writing is fun. After all, he doesn't have to do it. And by and large it has been not only a successful but a fun partnership.

With one exception. We'd just finished Lucifer's Hammer (Fawcett Books), and it was mid-December; when came a blivet from our editor. Changes needed, saith he; and on examination we decided he was right. But the book was scheduled, and due at the printer in January, so there was nothing for it but to grind and grind hard; one of the few times Niven found himself under the pressures most writers experience constantly. And for nearly a year afterwards he complained that I'd cost him the Christmas season.

After Hammer *stayed fifteen weeks on the best-seller list he forgave me.*

You don't usually associate Larry Niven stories with the near future. He's more comfortable with a farther future, one containing Ringworlds and other immense structures. It took harrying to get him to produce this one.

A Golden Age means a lot of things to different people, and one characteristic is that most don't know when they're living in one. It's only later and by contrast that they recall the "good old days" or dimly remember that golden time when . . .

The people in "Cloak of Anarchy" discover that truth much faster than most, and they learn it the hard way.

cloak of anarchy

by larry niven

Square in the middle of what used to be the San Diego
Freeway, I leaned back against a huge, twisted oak.
The old bark was rough and powdery against my bare
back. There was a dark green shade shot with tight
parallel beams of white gold. Long grass tickled my
legs.

Forty yards away across a wide strip of lawn was a
clump of elms, and a small grandmotherly woman sitting on a green towel She looked like she'd grown
there. A stalk of grass protruded between her teeth. I
felt we were kindred spirits, and once when I caught
her eye I wiggled a forefinger at her, and she waved
back

In a minute now I'd have to be getting up. Jill was
meeting me at the Wilshire exits in half an hour. But
I'd started walking at the Sunset Boulevard ramps, and
I was tired. A minute more....

It was a good place to watch the world rotate.

A good day for it, too. No clouds at all. On this hot
blue summer afternoon, King's Free Park was as
crowded as it ever gets.

Someone at police headquarters had expected that.
Twice the usual number of copseyes floated overhead,
waiting. Gold dots against blue, basketball-sized, twelve
feet up. Each a television eye and a sonic stunner, each

a hookup to police headquarters, they were there to enforce the law of the park.

No violence.

No hand to be raised against another—and no other laws whatever. Life was often entertaining in a Free Park.

North toward Sunset, a man carried a white rectangular sign, blank on both sides. He was parading back and forth in front of a square-jawed youth on a plastic box, who was trying to lecture him on the subject of fusion power and the heat-pollution problem. Even this far away I could hear the conviction and the dedication in his voice.

South, a handful of yelling marksmen were throwing rocks at a copseye, directed by a gesticulating man with wild black hair. The golden basketball was dodging the rocks, but barely. Some cop was baiting them. I wondered where they had gotten the rocks. Rocks were scarce in King's Free Park.

The black-haired man looked familiar. I watched him and his horde chasing the copseye . . . then forgot them when a girl walked out of a clump of elms.

She was lovely. Long, perfect legs, deep red hair worn longer than shoulder length, the face of an arrogant angel, and a body so perfect that it seemed unreal, like an adolescent's daydream. Her walk showed training; possibly she was a model or dancer. Her only garment was a cloak of glowing blue velvet.

It was fifteen yards long, that cloak. It trailed back from two big gold discs that were stuck somehow to the skin of her shoulders. It trailed back and back, floating at a height of five feet all the way, twisting and turning to trace her path through the trees. She seemed like the illustration to a book of fairy tales, bearing in mind that the original fairy tales were not intended for children.

Neither was she. You could hear neck vertebrae popping all over the park. Even the rock throwers had stopped to watch.

She could sense the attention, or hear it in a whisper of sighs. It was what she was here for. She strolled along with a condescending angel's smile on her angel's face, not overdoing the walk, but letting it flow. She turned regardless of whether there were obstacles to avoid, so that fifteen yards of flowing cloak could follow the curve.

I smiled, watching her go. She was lovely from the back, with dimples.

The man who stepped up to her a little further on was the same who had led the rock throwers. Wild black hair and beard, hollow cheeks and deep-set eyes, a diffident smile and a diffident walk . . . Ron Cole. Of course.

I didn't hear what he said to the girl in the cloak, but I saw the result. He flinched, then turned abruptly and walked away with his eyes on his feet.

I got up and moved to intercept him. "Don't take it personally," I said.

He looked up, startled. His voice, when it came, was bitter. "How should I take it?"

"She'd have turned any man off the same way. That lady has staples in her navel. She's to look, not to touch."

"You know her?"

"Never saw her before in my life."

"Then—?"

"Her cloak. Now you *must* have noticed the cloak."

The tail end of her cloak was just passing us, its folds

rippling an improbably deep, rich blue. Ronald Cole smiled as if it hurt his face. "Yah."

"All right. Now suppose you made a pass, and suppose the lady liked your looks and took you up on it. What would she do next? Bearing in mind that she can't stop walking even for a second."

He thought it over first, then asked, "Why not?"

"If she stops walking she loses the whole effect. Her cloak just hangs there like some kind of tail. It's supposed to wave. If she lies down with you it's even worse. A cloak floating at five feet, then swooping into a clump of bushes and bobbing frantically—" Ron laughed helplessly in falsetto. I said, "See? Her audience would get the giggles. That's not what she's after."

He sobered. "But if she really wanted to, she wouldn't *care* about . . . oh. Right. She must have spent a fortune to get that effect."

"Sure. She wouldn't ruin it for Jacques Casanova himself." I thought unfriendly thoughts toward the girl in the cloak. There are polite ways to turn down a pass. Ronald Cole was easy to hurt.

I asked, "Where did you get the rocks?"

"Rocks? Oh, we found a place where the center divider shows through. We knocked off some chunks of concrete." Ron looked down the length of the park as a kid bounced a missile off a golden ball. "They got one! Come on!"

The fastest commercial shipping that ever sailed was the clipper ship; yet the world stopped building them after just twenty-five years. Steam had come. Steam was faster, safer, more dependable, cheaper in time and men.

The freeways served America for almost fifty years. Then modern transportation systems cleaned the air and made traffic jams archaic and left the nation with an embarrassing problem. What to do with ten thousand miles of unsightly abandoned freeways?

King's Free Park had been part of the San Diego Freeway, the section between Sunset and the Santa Monica interchange. Decades ago the concrete had been covered with topsoil. The borders had been landscaped from the start. Now the park was as thoroughly covered with green as the much older Griffith Free Park.

Within King's Free Park was an orderly approximation of anarchy. People were searched at the entrances. There were no weapons inside. The copseyes, floating overhead and out of reach, were the next best thing to no law at all.

There was only one law to enforce. All acts of attempted violence carried the same penalty for attacker and victim. Let anyone raise his hand against his neighbor, and one of the golden basketballs would stun them both. They would wake separately, with copseyes watching. It was usually enough.

Naturally people threw rocks at copseyes. It was a Free Park, wasn't it?

"They got one! Come on!" Ron tugged at my arm. The felled copseye was hidden, surrounded by those who had destroyed it. "I hope they don't kick it apart. I told them I need it intact, but that might not stop them."

"It's a Free Park. And they bagged it."

"With my missiles!"

"Who are they?"

"I don't know. They were playing baseball when I found them. I told them I needed a copseye. They said they'd get me one."

I remembered Ron quite well now. Ronald Cole was an artist and an inventor. It would have been two sources of income for another man, but Ron was different. He invented new art forms. With solder and wire and diffraction gratings and several makes of plastics kits, and an incredible collection of serendipitous junk, Ron Cole made things the like of which had never been seen on Earth.

The market for new art forms has always been low, but now and then he did make a sale. It was enough to keep him in raw materials, especially since many of his raw materials came from basements and attics. There was an occasional *big* sale, and then, briefly, he would be rich.

There was this about him: he knew who I was, but he hadn't remembered my name. Ron Cole had better things to think about than what name belonged with whom. A name was only a tag and a conversational gambit. "Russel! How are you?" A signal. Ron had developed a substitute.

Into a momentary gap in the conversation he would say, "Look at this," and hold out—miracles.

Once it had been a clear plastic sphere, golf-ball sized, balanced on a polished silver concavity. When the ball rolled around on the curved mirror, the reflections were *fantastic*.

Once it had been a twisting sea serpent engraved on a Michelob beer bottle, the lovely vase-shaped bottle of the early 1960s that was too big for standard refrigerators.

And once it had been two strips of dull silvery metal, unexpectedly heavy. "What's this?"

I'd held them in the palm of my hand. They were heavier than lead. Platinum? But nobody carries that much platinum around. Joking, I'd asked, "U-235?"

"Are they warm?" he'd asked apprehensively. I'd fought off an urge to throw them as far as I could and dive behind a couch.

But they *had* been platinum. I never did learn why Ron was carrying them about. Something that didn't pan out.

Within a semicircle of spectators, the felled copseye lay on the grass. It was intact, possibly because two cheerful, conspicuously large men were standing over it, waving everyone back.

"Good," said Ron. He knelt above the golden sphere, turned it with his long artist's fingers. To me he said, "Help me get it open."

"What for? What are you after?"

"I'll tell you in a minute. Help me get—never mind." The hemispherical cover came off. For the first time ever, I looked into a copseye.

It was impressively simple. I picked out the stunner by its parabolic reflector, the cameras, and a toroidal coil that had to be part of the floater device. No power source. I guessed that the shell itself was a power-beam antenna. With the cover cracked there would be no way for a damn fool to electrocute himself.

Ron knelt and studied the strange guts of the copseye. From his pocket he took something made of glass and metal. He suddenly remembered my existence and held it out to me, saying, "Look at this."

I took it, expecting a surprise, and I got it. It was an old hunting watch, a big wind-up watch on a chain, with a protective case. They were in common use a couple of hundred years ago. I looked at the face, said, "Fifteen minutes slow. You didn't repair the whole works; did you?"

"Oh, no." He clicked the back open for me.

The works looked modern. I guessed, "Battery and tuning fork?"

"That's what the guard thought. Of course that's what I made it from. But the hands don't move; I set them just before they searched me."

"Aha. What does it do?"

"If I work it right, I think it'll knock down every copseye in King's Free Park."

For a minute or so I was laughing too hard to speak. Ron watched me with his head on one side, clearly wondering if I thought he was joking.

I managed to say, "That ought to cause all *kinds* of excitement."

Ron nodded vigorously. "Of course it all depends on whether they use the kind of circuits I think they use. Look for yourself; the copseyes aren't supposed to be foolproof. They're supposed to be cheap. If one gets knocked down, the taxes don't go up much. The other way is to make them expensive and foolproof, and frustrate a lot of people. People aren't supposed to be frustrated in a Free Park."

"So?"

"Well, there's a cheap way to make the circuitry for the power system. If they did it that way, I can blow the whole thing. We'll see." Ron pulled thin copper wire from the cuffs of his shirt.

"How long will this take?"

"Oh, half an hour."

That decided me. "I've got to be going. I'm meeting Jill Hayes at the Wilshire exits. You've met her, a big blonde girl, my height—"

But he wasn't listening. "Okay, see you," he muttered. He began placing the copper wire inside the copseye, with tweezers. I left.

Crowds tend to draw crowds. A few minutes after leaving Ron, I joined a semicircle of the curious to see what they were watching.

A balding, lantern-jawed individual was putting something together: an archaic machine, with blades and a small gasoline motor. The T-shaped wooden handle was brand new and unpainted. The metal parts were dull with the look of ancient rust recently removed.

The crowd speculated in half whispers. What was it? Not part of a car; not an outboard motor, though it had blades; too small for a motor scooter; too big for a motor skateboard . . .

"Lawn mower," said the white-haired lady next to me. She was one of those small, birdlike people who shrivel and grow weightless as they age, and live forever. Her words meant nothing to me. I was about to ask, when—

The lantern-jawed man finished his work, and twisted something, and the motor started with a roar. Black smoke puffed out. In triumph he gripped the handles. Outside, it was a prison offense to build a working internal combustion machine. Here—

With the fire of dedication burning in his eyes, he wheeled his infernal machine across the grass. He left a path as flat as a rug. It was a Free Park, wasn't it?

The smell hit everyone at once: a black dirt in the air, a stink of half-burned hydrocarbons attacking nose and eyes. I gasped and coughed. I'd never smelled anything like it.

The crescent of crowd roared and converged.

He squawked when they picked up his machine. Someone found a switch and stopped it. Two men confiscated the tool kit and went to work with screwdriver and hammer. The owner objected. He picked up a heavy pair of pliers and tried to commit murder.

A copseye zapped him and the man with the hammer, and they both hit the lawn without bouncing. The rest of them pulled the lawn mower apart and bent and broke the pieces.

"I'm half-sorry they did that," said the old woman. "Sometimes I miss the sound of lawn mowers. My dad used to mow the lawn on Sunday mornings."

I said, "It's a Free Park."

"Then why can't he build anything he pleases?"

"He can. He did. Anything he's free to build, we're free to kick apart." And my mind flashed, *Like Ron's rigged copseye.*

Ron was good with tools. It would not surprise me a bit if he knew enough about copseyes to knock out the whole system.

Maybe someone ought to stop him.

But knocking down copseyes wasn't illegal. It happened all the time. It was part of the freedom of the park. If Ron could knock them all down at once, well . . .

Maybe someone ought to stop him.

I passed a flock of high-school girls, all chittering like birds, all about sixteen. It might have been their first trip inside a Free Park. I looked back because they were so cute, and caught them staring in awe and wonder at the dragon on my back.

A few years and they'd be too blasé to notice. It had taken Jill almost half an hour to apply it this morning: a glorious red-and-gold dragon breathing flames across my shoulder, flames that seemed to glow by their own light. Lower down were a princess and a knight in golden armor, the princess tied to a stake, the knight fleeing for his life. I smiled back at the girls, and two of them waved.

Short blonde hair and golden skin, the tallest girl in sight, wearing not even a nudist's shoulder pouch: Jill Hayes stood squarely in front of the Wilshire entrance, visibly wondering where I was. It was five minutes after three.

There was this about living with a physical-culture nut. Jill insisted on getting me into shape. The daily exercises were part of that, and so was this business of walking half the length of King's Free Park.

I'd balked at doing it briskly, though. Who walks briskly in a Free Park? There's too much to see. She'd given me an hour; I'd held out for three. It was a compromise, like the paper slacks I was wearing despite Jill's nudist beliefs.

Sooner or later she'd find someone with muscles, or I'd relapse into laziness, and we'd split. Meanwhile . . . we got along. It seemed only sensible to let her finish my training.

She spotted me, yelled, "Russel! Here!" in a voice that must have reached both ends of the park. In answer I lifted my arm semaphore-style, slowly, over my head and back down.

And every copseye in King's Free Park fell out of the sky, dead.

Jill looked about her at all the startled faces and all the golden bubbles resting in bushes and on the grass. She approached me somewhat uncertainly. She asked, "Did you do that?"

I said, "Yah. If I wave my arms again they'll all go back up."

"I think you'd better do it," she said primly. Jill had a fine poker face. I waved my arm grandly over my head and down, but of course the copseyes stayed where they had fallen.

Jill said, "I wonder what happened to them?"

"It was Ron Cole. You remember him. He's the one who engraved some old Michelob beer bottles for Steuben—"

"Oh, yes. But *how?*"

We went off to ask him.

A brawny college man howled and charged past us at a dead run. We saw him kick a copseye like a soccer ball. The golden cover split, but the man howled again and hopped up and down hugging his foot.

We passed dented golden shells and broken resonators and bent parabolic reflectors. One woman looked flushed and proud; she was wearing several of the copper toroids as bracelets. A kid was collecting the cameras. Maybe he thought he could sell them outside.

I never saw an intact copseye after the first minute.

They weren't all busy kicking copseyes apart. Jill stared at the conservatively dressed group carrying POPULATION BY COPULATION signs, and wanted to know if they were serious. Their grim-faced leader handed us pamphlets that spoke of the evil and the blasphemy of man's attempts to alter himself through gene tampering and extrauterine-growth experiments. If it was a put-on, it was a good one.

We passed seven little men, each three to four feet high, traveling with a single tall, pretty brunette. They wore medieval garb. We both stared; but I was the one who noticed the makeup and the use of UnTan. African pigmies, probably part of a U.N.-sponsored tourist group; and the girl must be their guide.

Ron Cole was not where I had left him.

"He must have decided that discretion is the better part of cowardice. May be right, too," I surmised. "Nobody's ever knocked down *all* the copseyes before."

"It's not illegal, is it?"

"Not illegal, but excessive. They can bar him from the park, at the very least."

Jill stretched in the sun. She was all golden and *big*. Scaled down, she would have made a nice centershot for a men's videozine. She said, "I'm thirsty. Is there a fountain around?"

"Sure, unless someone's plugged it by now. It's a—"

"Free Park. Do you mean to tell me they don't even protect the *fountains?*"

"You make one exception, it's like a wedge. When someone ruins a fountain, they wait and fix it that night. That way if I see someone trying to wreck a fountain, I'll generally throw a punch at him. A lot of us do. After a guy's lost enough of his holiday to the copseye stunners, he'll get the idea, sooner or later."

The fountain was a solid cube of concrete with four spigots and a hand-sized metal button. It was hard to jam, hard to hurt. Ron Cole stood near it, looking lost.

He seemed glad to see me, but still lost. I introduced him. "You remember Jill Hayes." He said, "Certainly. Hello, Jill," and, having put her name to its intended purpose, promptly forgot it.

Jill said, "We thought you'd made a break for it."

"I did."

"Oh?"

"You know how complicated the exits are. They have to be, to keep anyone from getting in through an exit with like a shotgun." Ron ran both hands through his hair, without making it any more or less neat. "Well, all the exits have stopped working. They must be on the same circuits as the copseyes. I wasn't expecting that."

"Then we're locked in," I said. That was irritating.

But underneath the irritation was a funny feeling in the pit of my stomach. "How long do you think—?"

"No telling. They'll have to get new copseyes in somehow. And repair the beamed-power system, and figure out how I bollixed it, and fix it so it doesn't happen again. I suppose someone must have kicked my rigged copseye to pieces by now, but the police don't know that."

"Oh, they'll just send in some cops," said Jill.

"Look around you."

There were pieces of copseyes in all directions. Not one remained whole. A cop would have to be out of his mind to enter a Free Park.

Not to mention the damage to the spirit of the park.

"I wish I'd brought a bag lunch," said Ron.

I saw the cloak off to my right: a ribbon of glowing blue velvet hovering at five feet, like a carpeted path in the air. I didn't yell or point or anything. For Ron it might be pushing the wrong buttons.

Ron didn't see it. "Actually I'm kind of glad this happened," he said animatedly. "I've always thought that anarchy ought to be a viable form of society."

Jill made polite sounds of encouragement.

"After all, anarchy is only the last word in free enterprise. What can a government do for people that people can't do for themselves? Protection from other countries? If all the other countries are anarchies too, you don't need armies. Police, maybe; but what's wrong with privately owned police?"

"Fire departments used to work that way," Jill remembered. "They were hired by the insurance companies. They only protected houses that belonged to their own clients."

"Right! So you buy theft and murder insurance, and the insurance companies hire a police force. The client carries a credit card—"

"Suppose the robber steals the card too?"

"He can't use it. He doesn't have the right retina prints."

"But if the client doesn't have the credit card, he can't sic the cops on the thief."

"Oh." A noticeable pause. "Well—"

Half-listening, for I had heard it all before, I looked for the end points of the cloak. I found empty space at one end and a lovely red-haired girl at the other. She was talking to two men as outré as herself.

One can get the impression that a Free Park is one gigantic costume party. It isn't. Not one person in ten wears anything but street clothes, but the costumes are what get noticed.

These guys were part bird.

Their eyebrows and eyelashes were tiny feathers, green on one, golden on the other. Larger feathers covered their heads, blue and green and gold, and ran in a crest down their spines. They were bare to the waist, showing physiques Jill would find acceptable.

Ron was lecturing. "What does a government do for *anyone* except the people who run the government? Once there were private post offices, and they were cheaper than what we've got now. Anything the government takes over gets more expensive, *immediately*. There's no reason why private enterprise can't do anything a government—"

Jill gasped. She said, "Ooh! How lovely."

Ron turned to look.

As if on cue, the girl in the cloak slapped one of the feathered men hard across the mouth. She tried to hit the other one, but he caught her wrist. Then all three froze.

I said, "See? Nobody wins. She doesn't even like standing still. She—" And I realized why they weren't moving.

In a Free Park it's easy for a girl to turn down an offer. If the guy won't take no for an answer, he gets slapped. The stun beam gets him and the girl. When she wakes up, she walks away.

Simple.

The girl recovered first. She gasped and jerked her wrist loose and turned to run. One of the feathered men didn't bother to chase her; he simply took a double handful of the cloak.

This was getting serious.

The cloak jerked her sharply backward. She didn't hesitate. She reached for the big gold discs at her shoulders, ripped them loose, and ran on. The feathered men chased her, laughing.

The redhead wasn't laughing. She was running all-out. Two drops of blood ran down her shoulders. I thought of trying to stop the feathered men, decided in favor of it—but they were already past.

The cloak hung like a carpeted path in the air, empty at both ends.

Jill hugged herself uneasily. "Ron, just how does one go about hiring your private police force?"

"Well, you can't expect it to form spontaneously—"

"Let's try the entrances. Maybe we can get out."

It was slow to build. Everyone knew what a copseye did. Nobody thought it through. Two feathered men chasing a lovely nude? A pretty sight; and why interfere? If she didn't want to be chased, she need only—what? And nothing else had changed. The costumes, the people with causes, the people looking for causes, the peoplewatchers, the pranksters...

Blank Sign had joined the POPULATION BY COPULATION faction. His grass-stained pink street tunic jarred strangely with their conservative suits, but he showed no sign of mockery; his face was as preternaturally solemn as theirs. Nonetheless they did not seem glad of his company.

It was crowded near the Wilshire entrance. I saw enough bewildered and frustrated faces to guess that it was closed. The little vestibule area was so packed that we didn't even try to find out what was wrong with the doors.

"I don't think we ought to stay here," Jill said uneasily.

I noticed the way she was hugging herself. "Are you cold?"

"No." She shivered. "But I wish I were dressed."

"How about a strip of that velvet cloak?"

"Good!"

We were too late. The cloak was gone.

It was a warm September day, near sunset. Clad only in paper slacks, I was not cold in the least. I said, "Take my slacks."

"No, hon, I'm the nudist." But Jill hugged herself with both arms.

"Here," said Ron, and handed her his sweater. She flashed him a grateful look, then, clearly embarrassed, she wrapped the sweater around her waist and knotted the sleeves.

Ron didn't get it at all. I asked him, "Do you know the difference between nude and naked?"

He shook his head.

"Nude is artistic. Naked is defenseless."

Nudity was popular in a Free Park. That night, na
kedness was not. There must have been pieces of that
cloak all over King's Free Park. I saw at least four that
night: one worn as a kilt, two being used as crude sa
rongs, and one as a bandage.

On a normal day, the entrances to King's Free Park
close at six. Those who want to stay, stay as long as
they like. Usually they are not many, because there
are no lights to be broken in a Free Park; but light
does seep in from the city beyond. The copseyes float
about, guided by infrared, but most of them are not
manned.

Tonight would be different.

It was after sunset, but still light. A small and an
cient lady came stumping toward us with a look of
murder on her lined face. At first I thought it was
meant for us, but that wasn't it. She was so mad she
couldn't see straight.

She saw my feet and looked up. "Oh, it's you. The
one who helped break the lawn mower," she said; which
was unjust. "A Free Park, is it? A Free Park! Two men
just took away my dinner!"

I spread my hands. "I'm sorry. I really am. If you
still had it, we could try to talk you into sharing it."

She lost some of her mad, which brought her em
barrassingly close to tears. "Then we're all hungry to
gether. I brought it in a plastic bag. Next time I'll use
something that isn't transparent, by d-damn!" She no
ticed Jill and her improvised sweater-skirt, and added,
"I'm sorry, dear, I gave my towel to a girl who needed
it even more."

"Thank you anyway."

"Please, may I stay with you people until the cops-

eyes start working again? I don't feel safe, somehow.
I'm Glenda Hawthorne."

We introduced ourselves. Glenda Hawthorne shook
our hands. By now it was quite dark. We couldn't see
the city beyond the high green hedges, but the change
was startling when the lights of Westwood and Santa
Monica flashed on.

The police were taking their own good time getting
us some copseyes.

We reached the grassy field sometimes used by the
Society for Creative Anachronism for their tourna-
ments. They fight on foot with weighted and padded
weapons designed to behave like swords, broadaxes,
morningstars, etc. The weapons are bugged so that they
won't fall into the wrong hands. The field is big and
flat and bare of trees, sloping upward at the edges.

On one of the slopes, something moved.

I stopped. It didn't move again, but it showed clearly
in light reflected down from the white clouds. I made
out something man-shaped and faintly pink, and a pale
rectangle nearby.

I spoke low. "Stay here."

Jill said, "Don't be silly. There's nothing for anyone
to hide under. Come on."

The blank sign was bent and marked with shoe
prints. The man who had been carrying it looked up
at us with pain in his eyes. Drying blood ran from his
nose. With effort he whispered, "I think they dislocated
my shoulder."

"Let me look." Jill bent over him. She probed him
a bit, then set herself and pulled hard and steadily on
his arm. Blank Sign yelled in pain and despair.

"That'll do it." Jill sounded satisfied. "How does it
feel?"

"It doesn't hurt as much." He smiled, almost.

"What happened?"

"They started pushing me and kicking me to make me go away. I was *doing* it, I was walking away. I *was*. Then one of the sons of bitches snatched away my sign—" He stopped for a moment, then went off at a tangent. "I wasn't hurting anyone with my sign. I'm a psych major. I'm writing a thesis on what people read into a blank sign. Like the blank sheets in the Rorschach tests."

"What kind of reactions do you get?"

"Usually hostile. But nothing like *that*." Blank Sign sounded bewildered. "Wouldn't you think a Free Park is the one place you'd find freedom of speech?"

Jill wiped at his face with a tissue from Glenda Hawthorne's purse. She said, "Especially when you're not saying anything. Hey, Ron, tell us more about your government by anarchy."

Ron cleared his throat. "I hope you're not judging it by *this*. King's Free Park hasn't been an anarchy for more than a couple of hours. It needs time to develop."

Glenda Hawthorne and Blank Sign must have wondered what the hell he was talking about. I wished him joy in explaining it to them, and wondered if he would explain who had knocked down the copseyes.

This field would be a good place to spend the night. It was open, with no cover and no shadows, no way for anyone to sneak up on us.

We lay on wet grass, sometimes dozing, sometimes talking. Two other groups no bigger than ours occupied the jousting field. They kept their distance; we kept ours. Now and then we heard voices, and knew that they were not asleep; not all at once, anyway.

Blank Sign dozed restlessly. His ribs were giving

him trouble, though Jill said none of them were broken. Every so often he whimpered and tried to move and woke himself up. Then he had to hold himself still until he fell asleep again.

"Money," said Jill. "It takes a government to print money."

"But you could get I.O.U.'s printed. Standard denominations, printed for a fee and notarized. Backed by your good name."

Jill laughed softly. "Thought of everything, haven't you? You couldn't travel very far that way."

"Credit cards, then."

I had stopped believing in Ron's anarchy. I said "Ron, remember the girl in the long blue cloak?"

A little gap of silence. "Yah?"

"Pretty, wasn't she? Fun to watch."

"Granted."

"If there weren't any laws to stop you from raping her, she'd be muffled to the ears in a long dress and carrying a tear-gas pen. What fun would that be? I *like* the nude look. Look how fast it disappeared after the copseyes fell."

"Mmm," said Ron.

The night was turning cold. Faraway voices, occasional distant shouts, came like thin gray threads in a black tapestry of silence. Mrs. Hawthorne spoke into that silence.

"What was that boy really saying with his blank sign?"

"He wasn't saying anything," said Jill.

"Now, just a minute, dear. I think he was, even if he didn't know it." Mrs. Hawthorne talked slowly, using the words to shape her thoughts. "Once there was an organization to protest the forced-contraception bill.

I was one of them. We carried signs for hours at a time.
We printed leaflets. We stopped people passing so that
we could talk to them. We gave up our time, we went
to considerable trouble and expense, because we wanted
to get our ideas across.

"Now, if a man had joined us with a blank sign, he
would have been *saying* something.

"His sign says that he has no opinion. If he joins us
he says that we have no opinion either. He's saying
our opinions aren't worth anything."

I said, "Tell him when he wakes up. He can put it
in his notebook."

"But his notebook is *wrong*. He wouldn't push his
blank sign in among people he agreed with, would he?"

"Maybe not."

"I . . . suppose I don't like people with no opinions."
Mrs. Hawthorne stood up. She had been sitting tailor-
fashion for some hours. "Do you know if there's a pop
machine nearby?"

There wasn't, of course. No private company would
risk getting their machines smashed once or twice a
day. But she had reminded the rest of us that we were
thirsty. Eventually we all got up and trooped away in
the direction of the fountain.

All but Blank Sign.

I'd *liked* that blank sign gag. How odd, how ominous,
that so basic a right as freedom of speech could depend
on so slight a thing as a floating copseye.

I was thirsty.

The park was bright by city light, crossed by sharp-
edged shadows. In such light it seems that one can see
much more than he really can. I could see into every
shadow; but, though there were stirrings all around us,
I could see nobody until he moved. We four, sitting

under an oak with our backs to the tremendous trunk must be invisible from any distance.

We talked little. The park was quiet except for occasional laughter from the fountain.

I couldn't forget my thirst. I could feel others being thirsty around me. The fountain was right out there in the open, a solid block of concrete with five men around it.

They were dressed alike in paper shorts with big pockets. They looked alike: like first-string athletes. Maybe they belonged to the same order or frat or R.O.T.C. class.

They had taken over the fountain.

When someone came to get a drink, the tall ash-blond one would step forward with his arm held stiffly out, palm forward. He had a wide mouth and a grin that might otherwise have been infectious, and a deep, echoing voice. He would intone, "Go back. None may pass here but the immortal Cthuthu," or something equally silly.

Trouble was, they weren't kidding. Or: They were kidding, but they wouldn't let anyone have a drink.

When we arrived, a girl dressed in a towel had been trying to talk some sense into them. It hadn't worked. It might even have boosted their egos: a lovely half-naked girl begging them for water. Eventually she'd given up and gone away.

In that light her hair might have been red. I hoped it was the girl in the cloak. She'd sounded healthy ...unhurt.

And a beefy man in a yellow business jumper had made the mistake of demanding his rights. It was not a night for rights. The blond kid had goaded him into screaming insults, a stream of unimaginative profanity, which ended when he tried to hit the blond kid.

Then three of them had swarmed over him. The man had left crawling, moaning of police and lawsuits.

Why hadn't somebody done something?

I had watched it all from sitting position. I could list my own reasons. One: it was hard to face the fact that a copseye would not zap them both, any second now. Two: I didn't like the screaming fat man much. He talked dirty. Three: I'd been waiting for someone else to step in.

As with the girl in the cloak. Damn it.

Mrs. Hawthorne said, "Ronald, what time is it?"

Ron may have been the only man in King's Free Park who knew the time. People generally left their valuables in lockers at the entrances. But years ago, when Ron was flush with money from the sale of the engraved beer bottles, he'd bought an implant-watch. He told time by one red mark and two red lines glowing beneath the skin of his wrist.

We had put the women between us, but I saw the motion as he glanced at his wrist. "Quarter of twelve."

"Don't you think they'll get bored and go away? It's been twenty minutes since anyone tried to get a drink," Mrs. Hawthorne said plaintively.

Jill shifted against me in the dark. "They can't be any more bored than we are. I think they'll get bored and stay anyway. Besides—" She stopped.

I said, "Besides that, we're thirsty *now*."

"Right."

"Ron, have you seen any sign of those rock throwers you collected? Especially the one who knocked down the copseye."

"No."

I wasn't surprised. In this darkness? "Do you remember his—" And I didn't even finish.

"Yes!" Ron said suddenly.

"You're kidding."

"No. His name was Bugeyes. You don't forget a name like that."

"I take it he had big, bulging eyes?"

"I didn't notice."

Well, it was worth a try. I stood and cupped my hands for a megaphone and shouted, *"Bugeyes!"*

One of the Water Monopoly shouted, "Let's keep the noise down out there!"

"Bugeyes!"

A chorus of remarks from the Water Monopoly. "Strange habits these peasants." "Most of them are just thirsty. *This* character—"

From off to the side: "What do you want?"

"We want to talk to you! Stay where you are!" To Ron I said, "Come on." To Jill and Mrs. Hawthorne, "Stay here. Don't get involved."

We moved out into the open space between us and Bugeyes's voice.

Two of the five kids came immediately to intercept us. They must have been bored, all right, and looking for action.

We ran for it. We reached the shadows of the trees before those two reached us. They stopped, laughing like maniacs, and moved back to the fountain.

A fourteen-year-old kid spoke behind us. "Ron?"

Ron and I, we lay on our bellies in the shadows of low bushes. Across too much shadowless grass, four men in paper shorts stood at parade rest at the four corners of the fountain. The fifth man watched for a victim.

A boy walked out between us into the moonlight.

His eyes were shining, big, expressive eyes, maybe a bit too prominent. His hands were big, too, with knobby knuckles. One hand was full of acorns.

He pitched them rapidly, one at a time, overhand. First one, then another of the Water Trust twitched and looked in our direction. Bugeyes kept throwing.

Quite suddenly, two of them started toward us at a run. Bugeyes kept throwing until they were almost on him; then he threw his acorns in a handful and dived into the shadows.

The two of them ran between us. We let the first go by: the wide-mouthed blond spokesman, his expression low and murderous now. The other was short and broad-shouldered, an intimidating silhouette seemingly all muscle. A tackle. I stood up in front of him, expecting him to stop in surprise; and he did, and I hit him in the mouth as hard as I could.

He stepped back in shock. Ron wrapped an arm around his throat.

He bucked. Instantly. Ron hung on. I did something I'd seen often enough on television: linked my fingers and brought both hands down on the back of his neck.

The blond spokesman should be back by now; and I turned, and he was. He was on me before I could get my hands up. We rolled on the ground, me with my arms pinned to my sides, him unable to use his hands without letting go. It was lousy planning for both of us. He was squeezing the breath out of me. Ron hovered over us, waiting for a chance to hit him.

Suddenly there were others, a lot of others. Three of them pulled the blond kid off me, and a beefy, bloody man in a yellow business jumper stepped forward and crowned him with a rock.

The blond kid went limp.

I was still trying to get my breath.

The man squared off and threw a straight left hook with the rock in his hand. The blond kid's head snapped back, fell forward.

I yelled, "Hey!" Jumped forward, got hold of the arm that held the rock.

Someone hit me solidly in the side of the neck.

I dropped. It felt like all my strings had been cut. Someone was helping me to my feet—Ron—voices babbling in whispers, one shouting, "Get him—"

I couldn't see the blond kid. The other one, the tackle, was up and staggering away. Shadows came from between the trees to play pileup on him. The woods were alive, and it was just a *little* patch of woods. Full of angry, thirsty people.

Bugeyes reappeared, grinning widely. "Now what? Go somewhere else and try it again?"

"Oh, no. It's getting very vicious out tonight. Ron, we've got to stop them. They'll kill him!"

"It's a Free Park. Can you stand now?"

"Ron, they'll *kill* him!"

The rest of the Water Trust was charging to the rescue. One of them had a tree branch with the leaves stripped off. Behind them, shadows converged on the fountain.

We fled.

I had to stop after a dozen paces. My head was trying to explode. Ron looked back anxiously, but I waved him on. Behind me the man with the branch broke through the trees and ran toward me to do murder.

Behind him, all the noise suddenly stopped.

I braced myself for the blow.

And fainted.

He was lying across my legs, with the branch still in his hand. Jill and Ron were pulling at my shoulders.

A pair of golden moons floated overhead.

I wriggled loose. I felt my head. It seemed intact.

Ron said, "The copseyes zapped him before he got to you."

"What about the others? Did they kill them?"

"I don't know." Ron ran his hands through his hair. "I was wrong. Anarchy isn't stable. It comes apart too easily."

"Well, don't do any more experiments, okay?"

People were beginning to stand up. They streamed towards the exits, gathering momentum, beneath the yellow gaze of the copseyes.

The character "Ron Cole" in Niven's story is based rather accurately on a mad genius of our acquaintance— a man who once paid back a loan to Larry with a check that somehow bounced, and in horror replaced it with a perfectly legal check drawn on a real bank account— but written on a check-sized sheet of thin gold. (He'd even got the weight just right: At the time, the gold was worth just a little more than the face value of the check.)

For some reason, this gentleman resented Larry's characterization of him in "Cloak of Anarchy," and challenged Larry to a duel, which was held in proper form; the seconds originally agreed to hand grenades in a clothes closet, but were persuaded by the principals to make that champagne corks at twenty paces. After three exchanges of fire, there were no casualties, but there was a lot of champagne to drink up. . . .

Harlan Ellison has discovered a secret path to riches.

Every writer eventually learns that if you're lucky you can sell everything about fifteen times: serial rights, anthology rights, put it into a story collection, sell it overseas . . . When you do research for a factual article you also plan a story using it as background. Adult novels turn into juveniles. All this cuts down on work and leaves time for the finer things like Newcastle Brown Ale.

Actually, Harlan doesn't drink, but he does have the business side of writing down to a fine art. Harlan sells everything. Once, forced to write a long letter demanding payment from an overdue publisher, Harlan fell into melancholy. Here he'd invested time in writing something that he wasn't going to get paid for. Then came inspiration.

He got on the phone and sold it to a business magazine as an example of a dunning letter. Someone once told me that Harlan Ellison is the only man in the world who can sell his used Kleenex, and I believe it.

He's also the only person I know who can produce perfectly publishable stories while sitting on a display in a store window; he once did that as part of a benefit. (It's a well-kept secret, but Harlan Ellison, despite his awesome reputation, is a very generous person.)

"Silent in Gehenna" does not postulate a rosy future. Where Bova sees us slowly grinding downhill into a morass of all-too-predictable problems, and Larry gives us a place to hide from the rulebook for a while, Harlan shows a future so bad that most of its inhabitants don't know it's grim.

silent in gehenna
by harlan ellison

Joe Bob Hickey had no astrological sign. Or rather,
more precisely, he had twelve. Every year he celebrated
his birthday under a different Pisces, Gemini, or Scor-
pio. Joe Bob Hickey was an orphan. He was also a
bastard. He had been found on the front porch of the
Sedgwick County, Kansas, Foundling Home. Wrapped
in a stained army blanket, he had been deserted on one
of the home's porch gliders. That was in 1992.

Years later, the matron who discovered him on the
porch remarked, looking into his eyes was like staring
down a hall with empty mirrors.

Joe Bob was an unruly child. In the home he seemed
to seek out trouble, in no matter what dark closet it
hid, and sink his teeth into it; nor would he turn it
loose, bloody and spent, till thunder crashed. Shunted
from foster home to foster home, he finally took off at
the age of thirteen, snarling. That was in 2005. Nobody
even offered to pack him peanut-butter sandwiches.
But after a while he was fourteen, then sixteen, then
eighteen, and by that time he had discovered what the
world was really all about, he had built muscle, he had
read books and tasted the rain, and on some road he
had found his purpose in life, and that was all right,
so he didn't have to worry about going back. And *fuck*
their peanut-butter sandwiches.

Joe Bob attached the jumper cable, making certain it was circled out far enough behind and around him to permit him sufficient crawl-space without snagging the bull. He pulled the heavy-wire snippers from his rucksack, cut the fence in the shape of a church window, returned the snips to the rucksack, slung it over one shoulder, and shrugged into it—once again reminding himself to figure out a new system of harness so the bullhorn and the rucksack didn't tangle.

Then, down on his gut, he pulled himself on elbows tight to his sides, through the electrified fence, onto the grounds of the University of Southern California. The lights from the guard towers never quite connected at this far corner of the quad. An overlooked blind spot. But he could see the state trooper in his tower to the left, tracking the area with the mini-radar unit. Joe Bob grinned. His bollixer was feeding back pussycat shape.

Digging his hands into the ground, frogging his legs, flatworm fellow, he did an Australian Crawl through the no man's land of the blind spot. Once, the trooper held in his direction, but the mini-radar picked up only feline and as curiosity paled and vanished, he moved on. Joe Bob slicked along smoothly. (*Lignum vitae*, owing to the diagonal and oblique arrangement of the successive layers of its fibers, cannot be split. Not only is it an incredibly tough wood—with a specific gravity of 1.333 it sinks in water—but, containing in its pores 26 percent of resin, it is lustrous and self-oiling. For this reason it was used as bearings in the engines of early ocean-going steamships.) Joe Bob as *lignum vitae*. Slicking along oily through the dark.

The Earth Sciences building—Esso Hall, intaglioed on a lintel—loomed up out of the light fog that wisped through the quadrangle, close to the ground. Joe Bob worked toward it, idly sucking at a cavity in a molar where a bit of stolen/fried/enjoyed chicken meat had lodged. There were trip-springs irregularly spaced around the building. Belly down, he did an elaborate flat-out slalom through them, performing his delicate calligraphy of passage. Then he was at the building, and he sat up, back to the wall, and unvelcro-ing the flap of a bandoleer pocket.

Plastique.

Outdated, in these times of sonic explosives and mist, but effective nonetheless. He planted his charges.

Then he moved on to the Tactics Building, the Bacteriophage Labs, the Central Records Computer block, and the Armory. Charged all.

Then he pulledcrawled back to the fence, unshipped the bullhorn, settled himself low so he made no silhouette against the yawning dawn just tingeing itself lightly in the East, and tripped the charges.

The Labs went up first, throwing walls and ceilings skyward in a series of explosions that ranged through the spectrum from blue to red and back again. Then the Computer Block shrieked and died, fizzing and sparking like a dust-circuit killing negative particles; then together the Earth Sciences and Tactics Buildings thundered like saurians and fell in on themselves, spuming dust and lath and plaster and extruded wall dividers and shards of melting metal. And, at last, the Armory, in a series of moist poundings that locked one after the other in a stately, yet irregular rhythm. And one enormous Olympian bang that blew the Armory to pieces filling the night with the starburst trails of tracer lightning.

It was all burning, small explosions continuing to firecracker amid the rising sound of students and faculty and troops scurrying through the debacle. It was all burning as Joe Bob turned the gain full on the bull and put it to his mouth and began shouting his message.

"You call this academic freedom, you bunch of earthworms! You call electrified fences and armed guards in your classrooms the path to learning? Rise you, you toadstools. Strike a blow for freedom."

The bollixer was buzzing, reporting touches from radar probes. It was feeding back mass shape, indistinct lumps, ground swells, anything. Joe Bob kept shouting.

"Grab their guns away from them." His voice boomed like the day of judgment. It climbed over the sounds of men trying to save other buildings and it thundered against the rising dawn. "Throw the troops off campus. Jefferson said, 'People get pretty much the kind of government they deserve.' Is *this* what you deserve!"

The buzzing was getting louder, the pulses coming closer together. They were narrowing the field on him. Soon they would have him pinned; at least with high probability. Then the squirt squads would come looking for him.

"Off the troops!

"There's still time. As long as *one* of you isn't all the way brainwashed, there's a chance. *You are not alone!* We are a large, organized resistance movement . . . come join us . . . trash their barracks . . . bomb their armories . . . off the Fascist varks! Freedom is now, grab it, while they're chasing their tails. Off the varks—"

The squirters had been positioned in likely sectors. When the mini-radar units triangulated, found a potential lurking place and locked, they were ready. His bollixer gave out one solid buzzing pulse, and he knew they'd locked on him. He slipped the bull back on its harness and fumbled for the flap of his holster. It came away with a velcro fabric-sound and he wrenched the squirt gun out. The wire-stock was folded across the body of the weapon and he snapped it open, locking it in place.

Get out of here, he told himself.

Shut up, he answered. *Off the varks!*

Hey, pass on that. I don't want to get killed.

Scared, mother chicken?

Yeah I'm scared. You want to get your ass shot up, that's craziness, you silly wimp. But don't take me with you!

The interior monologue came to an abrupt end. Off to Joe Bob's right three squirters came sliding through the crabgrass, firing as they came. It wouldn't have mattered, anyhow. Where Joe Bob went, Joe Bob went with.

The squirt charges hit the fence and popped, snicking, spattering, everywhere but the space Joe Bob had cut out in the shape of a church window. He yanked loose the jumper cable and jammed it into the rucksack, sliding backward on his stomach and firing over their heads.

I thought you were the bigger killer?

Shut up, damn you. I missed, that's all.

You missed, my tail. You just don't want to see blood.

Sliding, sliding, sculling backward, all arms and legs; and the squirts kept on coming. *We are a large, organized resistance movement,* he had bullhorned. He had lied. He was alone. He was the last. After him, there might not be another for a hundred years. Squirt charges tore raw gashes in the earth around him.

Scared! I don't want to get killed.

The chopper rose from over his sight horizon, rose

straight up and came on a dead line for his position. He heard a soft, whining sound and *Scared!* breezed through his mind again.

Gully. Down into it. Lying on his back, the angle of the grassy bank obscuring him from the chopper, but putting him blindside to the squirt squad. He breathed deeply, washed his lips with his tongue, too dry to help and he waited.

The chopper came right over and quivered as it turned for a strafing run. He braced the squirt gun against the bank of the gully and pulled the trigger, held it back as a solid line of charges raced up the air. He tracked ahead of the chopper, leading it. The machine moved directly into the path of fire. The first charges washed over the nose of the chopper, smearing the surface like oxidized chrome plate. Electrical storms, tiny whirlpools of energy flickered over the chopper, crazing the ports, blotting out the scene below to the pilot and his gunner. The squirt charges drank from the electrical output of the ship and drilled through the hull, struck the power source and the chopper suddenly exploded. Gouts of twisted metal, still flickering with squirt life, rained down across the campus. The squirters went to ground, dug in, to escape the burning metal shrapnel.

With the sound of death still echoing, Joe Bob Hickey ran down the length of the gully, into the woods, and was gone.

It has been said before, and will be said again, but never as simply or humanely as Thoreau said it: "He serves the state best, who opposes the state most."

(Aluminum acetate, a chemical compound which, in the form of its natural salt, $Al(C_2H_3C_2)_3$, obtained as a white, water-soluble amorphous powder, is used chiefly in medicine as an astringent and as an anti-septic. In the form of its basic salt, obtained as a white, crystalline, water-insoluble powder, it is used chiefly in the textile industry as a waterproofing agent, as a fireproofing agent, and as a mordant. A mordant can be several things, two of the most important being an adhesive substance for binding gold or silver leaf to a surface; and an acid or other corrosive substance used in etching to eat out the lines.)

Joe Bob Hickey as aluminum acetate. Mordant. Acid etching at a corroded surface.

Deep night found him in terrible pain, far from the burning ruin of the university. Stumbling beneath the gargantuan Soleri pylons of the continental tramway. Falling, striking, tumbling over and over in his stumbling. Down a gravel-bed into deep weeds and the smell of a sour creek. Hands came to him in the dark, and turned him face up. Light flickered and a voice said, "He's bleeding," and another voice, cracked and husky, said, "He's siding a squirter," and a third voice said, "Don't touch him, come on," and the first voice said again, "He's bleeding," and the light was applied to the end of a cigar stub just as it burned down. And then there was a long deep darkness again.

Joe Bob began to hurt. How long he had been hurting he didn't know, but he realized it had been going on for some time. Then he opened his eyes, and saw fire-light dancing dimpling dimly in front of him. He was propped up against the base of a sumac tree. A hand came out of the mist that surrounded him, seemed to come right out of the fire, and a voice he had heard once before said, "Here. Take a suck on this." A plastic bottle of something hot was held to his lips, and another hand he could not see lifted his head slightly, and he drank. It was a kind of soupness that tasted of grass.

But it made him feel better.

"I used some of the shpritz from the can in your knapsack. Something got you pretty bad. Right across the back. You was bleeding pretty bad. Seems to be mending okay. That shpritz."

Joe Bob went back to sleep. Easier this time.

The campfire was out. He could see clearly what there was to see. Dawn was coming up. But how could that be . . . another dawn? Had he run all through the day, evading the varks sent to track him down? It had to be just that. Dawn, he had been crouched outside the fence, ready to trip the charges. He remembered that. And the explosions. And the squirt team, and the chopper, and—

He didn't want to think about things falling out of the sky, burning, sparking.

Running, a full day and a night of running. There had been pain. Terrible pain. He moved his body slightly, and felt the raw throb across his back. A piece of the burning chopper must have caught him as he fled; but he had kept going. And now he was here, somewhere else. Where? Filtered light, down through cool waiting trees.

He looked around the clearing. Shapes under blankets. Half a dozen, no, seven. And the campfire just smoldering embers now. He lay there, unable to move, and waited for the day.

The first one to rise was an old man with a dirty stipple of beard, perhaps three days' worth, and a poached egg for an eye. He limped over to Joe Bob— who had closed his eyes to slits—and stared at him. Then he reached down, adjusted the unraveling blanket, and turned to the cooling campfire.

He was building up the fire for breakfast when two of the others rolled out of their wrappings. One was quite tall, wearing a hook for a hand, and the other was as old as the first man. He was naked inside his blankets and hairless from head to foot. He was pink, very pink, and his skin was soft. He looked incongruous: the head of an old man, with the wrinkled, pink body of a week-old baby.

Of the other four, only one was normal, undamaged. Joe Bob thought that till he realized the normal one was incapable of speech. The remaining three were a hunchback with a plastic dome on his back that flickered and contained bands of color that shifted and changed hue with his moods; a black man with squirt burns down one entire side of his face, giving him the appearance of someone standing forever half in shadow; and a woman who might have been forty or seventy, it was impossible to tell, with one-inch-wide window strips in her wrists and ankles, whose joints seemed to bend in the directions opposite normal.

As Joe Bob lay watching surreptitiously, they washed as best they could, using water from a Lister bag, avoiding the scum-coated and bubbling water of the foul creek that crawled like an enormous gray potato slug through the clearing. Then the old man with the odd eye came to him and knelt down and pressed his palm again Joe Bob's cheek. Joe Bob opened his eyes.

"No fever. Good morning."

"Thanks," Joe Bob said. His mouth was dry.

"How about a cup of pretty good coffee with chickory?" The old man smiled. There were teeth missing.

Joe Bob nodded with difficulty. "Could you prop me up a little?" The old man called, "Walter . . . Marty. . . ." And the one who could not speak came to him, followed by the black man with the half-ivory face. They gently lifted Joe Bob into a sitting position. His back hurt terribly and every muscle in his body was stiff from having slept on the cold ground. The old man handed Joe Bob a plastic milk bottle half-filled with coffee. "There's no cream or sugar, I'm sorry," he said. Joe Bob smiled thanks and drank. It was very hot, but it was good. He felt it running down inside him, thinning into his capillaries.

"Where am I? What is this place?"

"N'vada," said the woman, coming over and hunkering down. She was wearing plowboy overalls chopped short to the calves, held together at the shoulders by pressure clips.

"Where in Nevada?" Joe Bob asked.

"Oh, about ten miles from Tonopah."

"Thanks for helping me."

"I dint have nothin' to do with it at all. Had my way, we'd've moved on already. This close to the tramway makes me nervous."

"Why?" He looked up; the aerial tramway, the least impressive of all Paolo Soleri's arcologies, and even by that comparison breathtaking, soared away to the horizon on the sweep-shaped arms of pylons that rose an eighth of a mile above them.

"Company bulls, is why. They ride cleanup, all up'n down this stretch. Lookin' for sabooters. Don't like the idea them thinkin' we's *that* kind."

Joe Bob felt nervous. The biggest patriots were on death row. Rape a child, murder seven women, blow the brains out of an old shopkeeper, that was acceptable; but be anti-country and the worst criminals wanted to wreak revenge. He thought of Greg, who had been beaten to death on Q's death row, waiting on appeal, by a vark-killer who'd sprayed a rush-hour crowd with a squirter, attempting to escape a drugstore robbery that had gone sour. The vark-killer had beaten

Greg's head in with a three-legged stool from his cell.
Whoever these people were, they weren't what *he* was.

"Bulls?" Joe Bob asked.

"How long you been onna dodge, boy?" asked the
incredibly tall one with the hook for a hand. "Bulls.
Troops. The Man."

The old man chuckled and slapped the tall one on
the thigh. "Paul, he's too young to know those words.
Those were our words. Now they call them. . . ."

Joe Bob linked into the hesitation. "Varks?"

"Yes, varks. Do you know where that came from?"

Joe Bob shook his head.

The old man settled down and started talking, and
as if he were talking to children around a hearth, the
others got comfortable and listened. "It comes from the
Dutch Afrikaan for earth-pig, or aardvark. They just
shortened it to vark, don't you see?"

He went on talking, telling stories of days when he
had been younger, of things that had happened, of their
country when it had been fresher. And Joe Bob listened. How the old man had gotten his poached egg in
a government medical shop, the same place Paul had
gotten his metal hook, the same place Walter had lost
his tongue and Marty had been done with the acid that
had turned him half-white in the face. The same sort
of medical shop where they had each suffered. But they
spoke of the turmoil that had ended in the land, and
how it was better for everyone, even for roaming bands
like theirs. And the old man called them bindlestiffs,
but Joe Bob knew whatever that meant it wasn't what
he was. He knew one other thing: it was *not* better.

"Do you play Monopoly?" the old man asked.

The hunchback, his plastic dome flickering in pas-
tels, scampered to a rollup and undid thongs and pulled

out a cardboard box that had been repaired many times. Then they showed Joe Bob how to play Monopoly. He lost quickly, gathering property seemed a stupid waste of time to him. He tried to speak to them about what was happening in America, about the inviolability of the Pentagon Trust, about the abolishment of the Supreme Court, about the way colleges trained only for the corporations or the Trust, about the central computer banks in Denver where everyone's identity and history were coded for instant arrest, if necessary. About all of it. But they knew that. They didn't think it was bad. They thought it kept the sabooters in their place so the country could be as good as it had always been.

"I have to go," Joe Bob said finally. "Thank you for helping me." It was a standoff: hate against gratitude.

They didn't ask him to stay with them. He hadn't expected it.

He walked up the gravel bank; he stood under the long bird-shadow of the aerial tramway that hurtled from coast-to-coast and from Gulf to Great Lakes; he looked up. It seemed free. But he knew it was anchored in the earth, deep in the earth, every tenth of a mile. It only *seemed* free, because Soleri had dreamed it that way. Art was not reality—it was only the appearance of reality.

He turned east. With no place to go but more of the same, he went anywhere. Till thunder crashed in whatever dark closet.

Convocation, at the State University of New York at Buffalo, was a catered affair. Catered by varks, troops, squirters, and (Joe Bob, looking down from a roof, added) bulls. The graduating class was eggboxed, divided into groups of no more than four, in cubicles with clear plastic walls. Unobstructed view of the screens on which the President Comptroller gave his address, but no trouble for the quellers if there was trouble. (There had been rumors of unrest, and even a one-page hectographed protest sheet tacked to the bulletin boards on campus.)

Joe Bob looked around with the opera glasses. He was checking the doggie guards.

Tenure and status among the faculty were indicated by the size, model, and armament of the doggie-guard robots that hovered, humming softly, just above and to the right shoulder of every administrator and professor. Joe Bob was looking for a 2013 Dictograph model with mist sprayers and squirt nozzles. Latest model...President Comptroller.

The latest model down there in the crowd was a 2007. That meant it was all assistant profs and teaching guides.

And *that* meant they were addressing the commencement exercises from the studio in the Ad Building. He slid back across the roof and into the gun tower. The guard was still sleeping, cocooned with spinex. He stared at the silver-webbed mummy. They would find him and spray him with dissolvent. Joe Bob had left the nose unwebbed; the guard could breathe.

Bigger killer.

Shut up.

Effective commando.

I told you to shut the hell up.

He slipped into the guard's one-piece stretchsuit, smoothed it down the arms to the wrists, stretching it to accommodate his broader shoulders. Then, carrying the harness and the rucksack, he descended the spiral staircase into the Ad Building proper. There were no varks in sight inside the building. They were all on perimeter detail; it was a high-caution alert: commencement day.

He continued down through the levels to the central heating system. It was June. Hot outside. The furnaces had been damped, the air conditioners turned on to a pleasant 71 degrees throughout the campus. He found the schematic for the ducts and traced the path to the studio with his fingers. He slipped into the harness and rucksack, pried open a grille, and climbed into the system. It was a long, vertical climb through the ductwork. Climbing. . . .

20 do you remember the rule that was passed into law, that nothing could be discussed in open classes that did not pertain directly to the subject matter being taught that day 19 and do you remember that modern art class in which you began asking questions about the uses of high art as vehicles for dissent and revolution 18 and how you began questioning the professor about Picasso's *Guernica* and what fever it had taken to paint it as a statement about the horrors of war 17 and how the professor had forgotten the rule and had recounted the story of Diego Rivera's Rockefeller Center fresco that had been commissioned by Nelson Rockefeller 16 and how, when the fresco was completed, Rivera had painted in Lenin prominently, and Rockefeller demanded another face he painted over it, and Rivera had refused 15 and how Rockefeller had had the fresco destroyed 14 and within ten minutes of the discussion the Comptroller had had the professor arrested 13 and do you remember the day the Pentagon Trust contributed the money to build the new stadium in exchange for the Games Theory department being converted to Tactics and they renamed the building Neumann Hall 12 and do you remember when you registered for classes and they ran you through Central and

found all the affiliations and made you sign the loyalty oath for students 11 and the afternoon they raided the basement 10 and caught you and Greg and Terry and Katherine 9 and they wouldn't give you a chance to get out and they filled the basement with mist 8 and they shot Terry through the mouth and Katherine 7 and Katherine 6 and Katherine 5 and she died folded up like a child on the sofa 4 and they came in and shot holes in the door from the inside so it looked like you'd been firing back at them 3 and they took you and Greg into custody 2 and the boot and the manacles and the confessions and you escaped and ran 1

Climbing—

Looking out through the interstices of the grille. The studio. Wasn't it fine. Cameras, sets, all of them—fat and powdered and happy. The doggies turning turning above their shoulders in the air turning and turning.

Now we find out just how tough you really are.

Don't start with me.

You've got to actually kill someone now.

I know what I've got to do.

Let's see how your peace talk sits with butchering someone—

Damn you!

—in cold blood, isn't that what they call it?

I can do it.

Sure you can. You make me sick.

I can: I can do it. I have to do it.

So do.

The studio was crowded with administrative officials, with technicians, with guards and troops, with mufti-laden military personnel looking over the graduating class for likely impressedmen. And in the campus brig, seventy feet beneath the Armory, eleven students crouched in maximum-security monkey cages:

unable to stand, unable to sit, built so a man could only crouch, spines bowed like bushmen in an outback.

With the doggies scanning, turning and observing, ready to fire, it was impossible to grab the President Comptroller. But there was a way to confound the robot guards. Wendell had found the way at Dartmouth, but he'd died for the knowledge. But there *was* a way.

If a man does the dying for you.

A vark. If a vark dies.

They die the same.

He ignored the conversation. It led nowhere; it never led anywhere but the same. The squirt gun was in his hands. He lay flat, spread his legs, feet turned out, and braced the wire stock against the hollow of his right shoulder. In the moment of light focused in the scope, he saw what would happen in the next seconds. He would squirt the guard standing beside the cameraman with the Arriflex. The guard would fall and the doggies would be alerted. They would begin scanning, and in that moment he would squirt one of them. It would short, and begin spraying. The other doggies would home in, begin firing among themselves, and in the ensuing confusion he would kick out the grille, drop down, and capture the Comptroller. If he was lucky. And if he was further lucky, he would get away with him. Further, and he would use him as ransom for the eleven.

Lucky. You'll die.

So I'll die. They die, I die. Both ways, I'm tired.

All your words, all your fine noble words.

He remembered all the things he had said through the bullhorn. They seemed far long lost and gone now. It was time for final moments. His finger tightened on the trigger.

The moment of light lengthened.

The light grew stronger.

He could not see the studio. The glare of the golden light blotted everything. He blinked, came out from behind the squirt gun, and realized the golden light was there with him, inside the duct, surrounding him, heating him, glowing and glowing. He tried to breathe and found he could not. His head began to throb, the pressure building in his temples. He had a fleeting thought—it was one of the doggies; he'd been sniffed out and this was some new kind of mist or a heat-ray or something new he hadn't known about. Then everything blurred out in a burst of golden brightness brighter than anything he had ever seen. Even lying on his back as a child, in a field of winter wheat, staring up with wide eyes at the sun, seeing how long he could endure. Why was it he had wanted to endure pain, to show whom? Even brighter than that.

Who am I and where am I going?

Who he was: uncounted billions of atoms, pulled apart and whirled away from there, down a golden tunnel bored in saffron space and ochre time.

Where he was going:

Joe Bob Hickey awoke and the first sensation of many that cascaded in on him was one of swaying. On a tideless tide, in air, perhaps water, swinging, back and forth, a pendulum movement that made him feel nauseous. Golden light filtered in behind his closed lids. And sounds. High musical sounds that seemed to cut off before he had heard them fully to the last vibrating tremolo. He opened his eyes and he was lying on his back on a soft surface that conformed to the shape of his body. He turned his head and saw the bullhorn and rucksack lying nearby. The squirt gun was gone. Then he turned his head back, and looked straight up. He had seen bars. Golden bars reaching in arcs toward a joining overhead. A cathedral effect, above him.

Slowly, he got to his knees, rolling tides of nausea moving in him. They were bars.

He stood up and felt the swaying more distinctly. He took three steps and found himself at the edge of the soft place. Set flush into the floor, it was a gray-toned surface, a huge circular shape. He stepped off, onto the solid floor of the . . . of the cage.

It *was* a cage.

He walked to the bars and looked out.

Fifty feet below was a street. A golden street on which great bulb-bodied creatures moved, driving before them smaller periwinkle blue humans, whipping them to push and pull the sitting carts on which the golden bulb creatures rode. He stood watching for a long time.

Then Joe Bob Hickey went back to the circular mattress and lay down. He closed his eyes and tried to sleep.

In the days that followed, he was fed well and learned that the weather was controlled. If it rained, an energy bubble—he didn't understand, but it was invisible—would cover his cage. The heat was never too great nor was he ever cold in the night. His clothes were taken away and brought back very quickly . . . changed. After that, they were always fresh and clean

He was someplace else. They let him know that much. The golden bulb-bodied creatures were the ruling class, and the smaller blue people-sorts were their workers. He was very someplace else.

Joe Bob Hickey watched the streets from his great

swaying cage, suspended fifty feet above the moving streets. In his cage he could see it all. He could see the golden bulb rulers as they drove the pitiful blue servants and he never saw the face of one of the smaller folk, for their eyes were constantly turned toward their feet.

He had no idea why he was there.

And he was certain he would stay there forever.

Whatever purpose they had borne in mind, to pluck him away from his time and place, they felt no need to impart to him. He was a thing in a cage—swinging free, in prison, high above a golden street.

Soon after he realized this was where he would spend the remainder of his life, he was bathed in a deep yellow light. It washed over him and warmed him, and he fell asleep for a while. When he awoke, he felt better than he had in years. The sharp pains the shrapnel wound had given him regularly had ceased. The wound had healed over completely. Though he ate the strange, simple foods he found in his cage, he never felt the need to urinate or void his bowels. He lived quietly, wanting for nothing, because he wanted nothing.

Get up, for God's sake. Look at yourself.

I'm just fine. I'm tired, let me alone.

He stood and walked to the bars. Down in the street, a golden bulb-creature's rolling cart had stopped almost directly under the cage. He watched as the blue people fell in the traces, and he watched as the golden bulb-thing beat them. For the first time, somehow, he saw it as he had seen things before he had been brought to this place. He felt anger at the injustice of it; he felt the blood hammering in his neck; he began screaming. The golden creature did not stop. Joe Bob looked for something to hurl. He grabbed the bullhorn and turned it on and began screaming, cursing, threatening the monster with the whip. The creature looked up and its many silver eyes fastened on Joe Bob Hickey. *Tyrant, killer, filth!* he screamed.

He could not stop. He screamed all the things he had screamed for years. And the creature stopped whipping the little blue people, and they slowly got to their feet and pulled the cart away, the creature following. When they were well away, the creature rolled once more onto the platform of the cart and whipped them.

"Rise up, you toadstools. Strike a blow for freedom."

He screamed all that day, the bullhorn throwing his voice away to shatter against the sides of the windowless golden buildings.

"Grab their whips away from them. Is *this* what you deserve. There's still time. As long as *one* of you isn't all the way beaten, there's a chance. *You are not alone.* We are a large, organized resistance movement...."

They aren't listening.

They'll hear.

Never. They don't care.

Yes. Yes, they do. Look. See?

And he was right. Down in the street, carts were pulling up and as they came within the sounds of his voice the golden bulb-creatures began wailing in terrible strident bug voices, and they beat themselves with the whips... and the carts started up again, pulled away... and the creatures beat their blue servants out of sight.

In front of him, they wailed and beat themselves, trying to atone for their cruelty. Beyond him, they resumed their lives.

It did not take him long to understand.

I'm their conscience.

You were the last they could find, and they took you, and now you hang up here and pillory them and they beat their breasts and wail mea culpa, mea maxima culpa, *and they purge themselves; then they go on as before.*

Ineffectual.

Totem.

Clown, I'm a clown.

But they had selected well. He could do no other. As he had always been a silent voice, screaming words that needed to be screamed, but never heard, so he was still a silent voice. Day after day they came below him, and wailed their guilt; and having done it were free to go on.

The deep yellow light, do you know what it did to you?

Yes.

Do you know how long you'll live, how long you'll tell them what filth they are, how long you'll sway here in this cage?

Yes.

But you'll still do it.

Yes.

Why? Do you like being pointless?

It isn't pointless.

Why not, you said it was, Why?

Because if I do it forever, maybe at the end of forever they'll let me die.

(The black-headed Gonolek is the most predatory of the African bush shrikes. Ornithologically, the vanga-shrikes occupy somewhat the same position among the passerines that the hawks and owls do among the non-passerines. Because they impale their prey on thorns, they have earned the ruthless name "butcherbird." Like many predators, shrikes often kill more than they can eat, and when opportunity presents itself seem to kill for the joy of killing.)

All was golden light and awareness.

(It is not uncommon to find a thorn tree or barbed-wire fence decorated with a dozen or more grasshoppers, locusts, mice, or small birds. That the shrikes establish such larders in times of plenty against future need has been questioned. They often fail to return, and the carcasses slowly shrivel or rot.)

Joe Bob Hickey, prey of his world, impaled on a thorn of light by the shrike, and brother to the shrike himself.

(Most bush shrikes have loud, melodious voices and reveal their presence by distinctive calls.)

He turned back to the street, putting the bullhorn to his mouth, and, alone as always, he screamed, "Jefferson said—"

This story comes close to violating the ground rules of this book, in that the ending is allegorical. I put that to Harlan and he informed me that (1) he could only too easily see the society he portrayed as growing out of the present, and (2) the ending was not allegorical at all, nor had he violated the ground rules.

You may interpret that however you choose

Poul Anderson is a most remarkable man. A graduate in physics, he keeps up with the scientific literature better than almost anyone in science fiction; better than most physics teachers.

In fact, there's very little that Poul can't do if he sets his mind to it—except, perhaps, get from the deck of my sailboat into the cabin without knocking over the lamp. In two cruises, one of well over a week, I don't believe he made it once.

He can, however, hang onto the tiller in gale-driven sleet for much of a night of full gale, so I can hardly begrudge him an occasional lamp chimney.

Poul is another who sees the people in 2020 looking back on 1980 as a Golden Age. We ought to be careful, he warns; eternal vigilance really is the price of liberty, and the watchmen are dozing. We might lose not only freedom, but its very memory—forever. "It's not us," he says, "that I weep for. We've had it pretty good, you and I and the rest of this generation. But we should cry for our children."

For obvious reasons I think of this story as one of a pair with Ellison's nightmare; and of the two, this is the one that frightens me. The world of "The Pugilist" is a Hell that we just might create for ourselves; a Hell without obvious exit. But even in Hell there is love. . . .

the pugilist

by poul anderson

They hadn't risked putting me in the base hospital or any other regular medical facility. Besides, the operation was very simple. Needed beforehand: a knife, an anesthetic, and a supply of coagulant and enzyme to promote healing inside a week. Needed afterward: drugs and skillful talking to, till I got over being dangerous to myself or my surroundings. The windows of my room were barred, I was brought soft plastic utensils with my meals, my clothes were pajamas and paper slippers, and two husky men sat in the hall near my open door. Probably I was also monitored on closed-circuit TV.

There was stuff to read, especially magazines which carried stories about the regeneration center in Moscow. Those articles bore down on the work being still largely experimental. A structure as complicated as a hand, a leg, or an eye wouldn't yet grow back right, though surgery helped. However, results were excellent with the more basic tissues and organs. I saw pics of a girl whose original liver got mercury poisoning, a man who'd had most of his skin burned off in an accident, beaming from the pages as good as new—or so the text claimed.

Mannix must have gone to some trouble to find those

issues. The latest was from months ago. You didn't see much now that wasn't related to the war.

Near the end of that week my male nurse gave me a letter from Bonnie. It was addressed to me right here, John Reed A.F.B., Willits, California 95491, in her own slanty-rounded handwriting, and according to the postmark—when I remembered to check that several hours later—had doubtless been mailed from our place, not thirty kilometers away. The envelope was stamped EXAMINED, but I didn't think the letter had been dictated. It was too her. About how the kids and the roses were doing, and the co-op where she worked was hoping the Recreation Bureau would okay its employees vacationing at Lake Pillsbury this year, and hamburger had been available day before yesterday and she'd spent three hours with her grandmother's old cookbook deciding how to fix it "and if only you'd been across the table, you and your funny slow smile; oh, do finish soon, Jim-Jim, and c'mon home."

I read slowly, the first few times. My hands shook so much. Later I crawled into bed and pulled the sheet over my face against bugeyes.

Mannix arrived next morning. He was small and chipper, always in the neatest of civies, his round red face always amiable—almost always—under a fluff of white hair. "Well, how are you, Colonel Dowling?" he exclaimed as he bounced in. The door didn't close behind him at once. My guards would watch a while. I stand 190 centimeters in my bare feet and black belt.

I didn't rise from my armchair, though. Wasn't sure I could. It was as if that scalpel had, actually, teased the bones out of me. The windows stood open to a cool breeze and a bright sky. Beyond the neat buildings and electric fence of the base, I could see hills green with forest roll up and up toward the blueness of the sierra. It felt like painted scenery. Bonnie acts in civic theater.

Mannix settled on the edge of my bed. "Dr. Arneson tells me you can be discharged anytime, fit for any duty," he said. "Congratulations."

"Yeah," I managed to say, though I could hear how feeble the sarcasm was. "You'll send me right back to my office."

"Or to your family? You have a charming wife."

I stirred and made a noise. The guard in the entrance looked uneasy and dropped a hand to his stunner. Mannix lifted a palm. "If you please," he chirped. "I'm not baiting you. Your case presents certain difficulties, as you well know."

I'd imagined I was calm, but numb. I was wrong. Blackness took me in a wave that roared. "Why, why, why?" I felt rip my throat. "Why not just shoot me and be done?"

Mannix waited till I sank back. The wind whined in and out of me. Sweat plastered the pajamas to my skin. It reeked.

He offered me a cigarette. At first I ignored him, then accepted both it and the flare of his lighter, and dragged my lungs full of acridness. Mannix said mildly, "The surgical procedure was necessary, Colonel. You were told that. Diagnosis showed cancer."

"The f-f-f—the hell it did," I croaked.

"I believe the removed part is still in alcohol in the laboratory," Mannix said. "Would you like to see it?"

I touched the hot end of the cigarette to the back of my hand. "No," I answered.

"And," Mannix said, "regeneration is possible."

"In Moscow."

"True, the Lomonosov institute has the world's only

such capability to date. I daresay you've been reading about that." He nodded at the gay-colored covers on the end table. "The idea was to give you hope. Still . . . you are an intelligent, technically educated man. You realize it isn't simple to make the adult DNA repeat what it did in the fetus; and not repeat identically, either. Not only are chemicals, catalysts, synthevirus required; the whole process must be monitored and computer-controlled. No wonder they concentrate on research and save clinical treatment for the most urgent cases." He paused. "Or the most deserving."

"I saw this coming," I mumbled.

Mannix shrugged. "Well, when you are charged with treasonable conspiracy against the People's Republic of the United States—" That was one phrase he had to roll out in full every time.

"You haven't proved anything," I said mechanically.

"The fact of your immunity to the usual interrogation techniques is, shall we say, indicative." He grew arch again. "Consider your own self-interest. Let the war in the Soviet Union break into uncontrolled violence, and where is Moscow? Where's the Institute? The matter is quite vital, Colonel."

"What can I do?" I asked out of hollowness.

Mannix chuckled. "Depends on what you know, what you are. Tell me and we'll lay plans. Eh?" He cocked his head. Bonnie, who knew him merely as a political officer, to be invited to dinner now and then on that account, liked him. She said he ought to play the reformed Scrooge, except he'd be no good as the earlier, capitalist Scrooge, before the Spirits of the New Year visited him.

"I've been studying your file personally," he went on, "and I'm blessed if I can see why you should have gotten involved in this unsavory business. A fine young man who's galloped through his promotions at the rate you have. It's not as if your background held anything un-American. How did you ever get sucked in?"

He bore down a little on the word "sucked." That broke me.

I'd never guessed how delicious it is to let go, to admit—fully admit and take into you—the fact that you're whipped. It was like, well, like the nightly surrender to Bonnie. I wanted to laugh and cry and kiss the old man's hands. Instead, stupidly, all I could say was, "I don't know."

The answer must lie deep in my past.

I was a country boy, raised in the backwoods of Georgia, red earth, gaunt murky-green pines, cardinals and mockingbirds and a secret fishing hole. The government had tried to modernize our area before I was born, but it didn't lend itself to collectives. So mostly we were allowed to keep our small farms, stores, sawmills, and repair shops on leasehold. The schools got taped lectures on history, ideology, and the rest. However, this isn't the same as having trained political educators in the flesh. Likewise, our local scoutmaster was lax about everything except woodcraft. And, while my grandfather mumbled a little about damn niggers everywhere like nothing since Reconstruction, he used to play poker with black Sheriff Jackson. Sometimes he, Granddad that is, would take on a bit too much moon and rant about how poor, decent Joe Jackson was being used. My parents saw to it that no outsiders heard him.

All in all, we lived in a pretty archaic fashion. I understand the section has since been brought up to date.

Now, patriotism is as Southern as hominy grits. They have trouble realizing this further north. They

harp on the Confederate Rebellion, though actually—
as our teachers explained to us—folks in those days
were resisting Yankee capitalism and the slaveholders
were a minority who milked the common man's love
for his land. True, when the People's Republic was pro-
claimed, there was some hothead talk, even some shooting. But there was never any need for the heavy concentration of marshals and deputies they sent down to
our states. Damn it, we still belonged.

We were the topmost rejoicers when word came: the
Treaty of Berlin was amended, the United States could
maintain armed forces well above police level, and was
welcomed to the solid front of Peace-loving nations
against the Sino-Japanese revisionists.

Granddad turned into a wild man in a stiff jacket.
He'd fought for the imperalist regime once, when it
tried to suppress the Mekong Revolution, though he
never said a lot about that. Who would? (I suppose Dad
was lucky, just ten years old at the time of the Sacred
War, which thus to him was like a hurricane or some
other natural spasm. Of course, the hungry years afterward stunted his growth.) "This's the first step!"
Granddad cried to us. "The first step back! You hear?"
He stood outdoors waving his cane, autumn sumac a
shout of red behind him, and the wind shouted, too, till
I imagined old bugles blowing again at Valley Forge
and Shiloh and Omaha Beach. Maybe that was when
I first thought I might make the Army a career.

A year later, units of the new service held maneu-
vers beneath Stone Mountain. Granddad had been tire-
lessly reading and watching news, writing letters,
making phone calls from the village booth, keeping in
touch. Hence he knew about the event well in advance,
knew the public would be invited to watch from certain

areas, and saved his money and his travel allowance till he could not only go himself but take me along.

And it was exciting, oh, yes, really beautiful when the troops went by in ground-effect carriers like magic boats, the dinosaur tanks rumbling past, the superjets screaming low overhead, while the Star and Stripes waved before those riders carved in the face of the mountain.

Except—the artillery opened up. Granddad and I were quite a ways off, the guns were toys in our eyes, we'd see a needle-thin flash, a puff where the shell exploded; long, long afterward, distance-shruken thunder reached us. The monument was slow to crumble away. That night, in the tourist dorm, I heard a speech about how destroying that symbol of oppression marked the dawn of our glorious new day. I didn't pay much attention. I kept seeing Granddad there, under the Georgia sky, suddenly withered and old.

Nobody proposed I go home to Bonnie. Least of all myself. Whether or not I could have made an excuse for ... not revealing to her what had happened ... I couldn't have endured it. I did say, over and over, that she had no idea I was in the Stephen Decatur Society. This was true. Not that she would have betrayed me had she known, Bonnie whose heart was as bright as her hair. I was already too far in to back out when first we met, too weak and selfish to run from her; but I was never guilty of giving her guilty knowledge.

"She and your children must have had indications," Mannix murmured. "If only subliminal. They might be in need of correctional instruction."

I whimpered before him. There are camps and camps, of course, but La Pasionara is the usual one for

West Coast offenders. I've met a few of those who've been released from it. They are terribly obedient, hard-working, and close-mouthed. Most lack teeth. Rumor says conditions can make young girls go directly from puberty to menopause. I have a daughter.

Mannix smiled. "At ease, Jim. Your family's departure would tip off the Society."

I blubbered my thanks.

"And, to be sure, you may be granted a chance to win pardon, if we can find a proper way," he soothed me. "Suggestions?"

"I-I-I can tell you . . . what I know—"

"An unimaginative minimum. Let us explore you for a start. Maybe we'll hit on a unique deed you can do." Mannix drummed his desktop.

We had moved to his office, which was lush enough that the portraits of Lennin and the President looked startlingly austere. I sat snug and warm in a water chair, cigarettes, coffee, brandy at hand, nobody before me or behind me except this kindly white-haired man and his recorder. But I was still gulping, sniffling, choking, and shivering, still too dazed to think. My lips tingled and my body felt slack and heavy.

"What brought you into the gang, Jim?" he asked as if in simple curiosity.

I gaped at him. I'd told him I didn't know. But maybe I did. Slowly I groped around in my head. The roots of everything go back to before you were born.

I'd inquired about the origins of the organization, in my early days with it. Nobody knew much except that it hadn't been important before Sotomayor took the leadership—whoever, wherever he was. Until him, it was a spontaneous thing.

Probably it hadn't begun right after the Sacred War. Americans had done little except pick up pieces, those first years. They were too stunned when the Soviet missiles knocked out their second-strike capability and all at once their cities were hostages for the good behavior of their politicians and submarines. They were too relieved when no occupation followed, aside from inspectors and White House advisors who made sure the treaty limitations on armaments were observed. (Oh, several generals and the like were hanged as war criminals.) True, the Soviets had taken a beating from what U.S. nukes did get through, sufficient that they couldn't control China or, later, a China-sponsored Japanese S.S.R. The leniency shown Americans was not the less welcome for being due to a shortage of troops.

Oath-brothers had told me how they were attracted by the mutterings of friends and presently recruited, after Moscow informed Washington that John Halper would be an unacceptable candidate for President in the next election. Others joined in reaction against a collectivist sentiment whose growth was hothouse-forced by government, schools, and universities.

I remember how Granddad growled, on a day when we were alone in the woods and I'd asked him about that period.

"The old order was blamed for the war and the war's consequences, Jimmy. Militarists, capitalists, imperialists, racists, bourgeoisie. Nobody heard any different any more. Those who'd've argued weren't gettin' published or on the air, nothin'." He drew on his pipe. Muscles bunched in the angle of his jaw. "Yeah, everybody was bein' blamed—except the liberals who'd worked to lower our guard so their snug dreams wouldn't be interrupted, the conservatives who helped

'em so's to save a few wretched tax dollars, the radicals
who disrupted the country, the copouts who lifted no
finger—" The bit snapped between his teeth. He
stooped for the bowl and squinted at it ruefully while
his heel ground out the scattered ashes. At last he
sighed. "Don't forget what I've told you, Jimmy. But
bury it deep, like a seed."

I can't say if he was correct. My life was not his. I
wasn't born when the Constitutional Convention pro-
claimed the People's Republic. Nor did I ever take a
strong interest in politics.

In fact, my recruitment was glacier gradual. At West
Point I discovered step by step that my best friends
were those who wanted us to become a first-class power
again, not conquer anybody else, merely cut the Russian apron strings. . . . Clandestine bitching sessions,
winked at by our officers, slowly turned into clandestine meetings which hinted at eventual action. An illegal newsletter circulated. . . . After graduation and
assignment, I did trivial favors, covering up for this or
that comrade who might otherwise be in trouble, supplying bits of classified information to fellows who said
they were blocked from what they needed by stupid
bureaucrats, hearing till I believed it that the pro-
scribed and abhorred Stephen Decatur Society was not
counterrevolutionary, not fascist, simply patriotic and
misunderstood. . . .

The final commitment to something like that is
when you make an excuse to disappear for a month—
in my case, a backpacking trip with a couple of guys,
though my C.O. warned me that asocial furloughs
might hurt my career—and you get flitted to an un-
specified place where they induct you. One of the psy-
chotechs there explained that the treatment, drugs,

sleep deprivation, shock conditioning, the whole damnable works, meant more than installing a set of reflexes. Those guarantee you can't be made to blab involuntarily under serum or torture. But the suffering has a positive effect, too: it's a rite of passage. Afterward you can't likely be bribed either.

Likely. The figures may change on a man's price tag, but he never loses it.

I don't yet know how I was detected. A Decaturist courier had cautioned my cell about microminiature listeners which can be slipped a man in his food, operate off body heat, and take days to be eliminated. With my work load, both official on account of the crisis and after hours in preparing for our coup, I must have gotten careless.

Presumably, though, I was caught by luck rather than suspicion in a spot check. If the political police had identified any fair-sized number of conspirators, Mannix wouldn't be as anxious to use me as he was.

Jarred, I realized I hadn't responded to his last inquiry. "Sir," I begged, "honest, I'm no traitor. I wish our country had more voice in its own affairs. Nothing else."

"A Titoist." Recognizing my glance of dull surprise at the new word, he waved it off. "Never mind. I forgot they've reimproved the history texts since I was young. Let's stick to practical matters, then."

"I, I can . . . identify for you—those in my cell." Jack whose wife was pregnant, Bill who never spared everyday helpfulness, Tim. . . . "B-but there must be others on the base and in the area, and, well some of them must know *I* belong."

"Right." Mannix nodded. "We'll stay our hand as

regards those you have met. Mustn't alert the organization. It does seem to be efficient. That devil Sotomayor—well, let's get on."

He was patient. Hours went by before I could talk coherently.

At that time he had occasion to turn harsh. Leaning across his desk—the window behind framed him in night—he snapped: "You considered yourself a patriot. Nevertheless you plotted mutiny."

I cringed. "No, sir. Really. I mean, the idea was—was—"

"Was what?" In his apple face stood the eyes of Old Scrooge.

"Sir, when civil war breaks out in the Motherland—those Vasiliev and Kunin factions—"

"Party versus Army."

"What?" I don't know why I tried to argue. "Sir, last I heard, Vasiliev's got everything west of the, uh, Yenisei . . . millions of men under arms, effective control of West Europe—"

"You do not understand how to interpret events. The essential struggle is between those who are loyal to the principles of the Party, and those who would like substitute military dictatorship." His finger jabbed. "Like you, Dowling."

We had told each other in our secret meetings, we Decatur folk, better government by colonels than commissioners.

"No, sir, no, sir," I protested. "Look, I'm only a soldier. But I see . . . I smell the factions here, too . . . the air's rotten with plotting . . . and what about in Washington? I mean, do we *know* what orders we'll get, any day now? And what is the situation in Siberia?"

"You have repeatedly been informed—the front is stabilized and relatively quiet."

My wits weren't so shorted out that I hinted the official media might ever shade the truth. I did reply: "Sir, I'm a missileman. In the, uh, the opinion of every colleague I've talked with—most of them loyal, I'm certain—what stability the front has got is due to the fact both sides have ample rockets, lasers, the works. If they both cut loose, there'd be mutual wipeout. Unless we Americans . . . we hold the balance." Breath shuddered into me. "Who's going to order our birds targeted where?"

Mannix sat for a while that grew very quiet. I sat listening to my heart stutter. Weariness filled me like water fills a sponge. I wanted to crawl off and curl up in darkness, alone, more than I wanted Bonnie or my children or tomorrow's sunrise or that which had been taken from me. But I had to keep answering.

At last he asked, softly, almost mildly. "Is this your honest evaluation? Is this why you were in a conspiracy to seize control of the big weapons?"

"Yes, sir." A vacuum passed through me. I shook myself free of it. "Yes, sir. I think my belief—the belief of most men involved—is, uh, if a, uh, a responsible group, led by experts, takes over the missile bases for the time being . . . those birds won't get misused. Like by, say, the wrong side in Washington pulling a coup—" I jerked my head upright.

"Your superiors in the cabal have claimed to you that the object is to keep the birds in their nests, keep America out of the war," Mannix said. "How do you know they've told you the truth?"

I thought I did. Did I? Was I? Big soft waves came rolling.

"Jim," Mannix said earnestly, "they've tricked you through your whole adult life. Nevertheless, what we've learned shows me you're important to them. You're slated for commander here at Reed, once the mutiny begins. I wouldn't be surprised but what they've been grooming you for years and that's how come your rapid rise in the services. Clues there—but as for now, you must have ways to get in touch with higher echelons."

"Uh-huh," I said. "Uh-huh. Uh-huh."

Mannix grew genial. "Let's discuss that, shall we?"

I don't remember being conducted to bed. What stands before me is how I woke, gasping for air, nothing in my eyes except night and nothing in the hand that grabbed at my groin.

I rolled over on my belly, clutched the pillow, and crammed it into my mouth. Bonnie, Bonnie, I said, they've left me this one way back to you. I pledge allegiance to you, Bonnie, and to the Chuck and Joanlet you have mothered, and *screw* the rest of the world!

("Even for a man in his thirties," said a hundred teachers, intellectuals, officials, entertainers out of my years, "or even for an adolescent, romantic atavism is downright unpatriotic. The most important thing in man's existence is his duty to the people and the molding of their future." The echoes went on and on.)

I've been a rat, I said to my three, to risk—and lose—the few things which counted, all of which were ours. Bonnie, it's no excuse for my staying with the Decaturists, that I'd see you turn white at this restriction or that command to volunteer service or yonder midnight vanishing of a neighbor. No excuse, nothing but a rationalization. I've led us down my rathole, and now my duty is to get us out in whatever way I am able.

("There should be little bloodshed," the liaison man told our cell; we were not shown his face. "The war is expected to remain stalemated for the several weeks we need. When the moment is right, our folk will rise, disarm and expel everybody who isn't with us, and dig in. We can hope to seize most of the rocket bases. Given the quick retargetability of every modern bird, we will then be in a position to hit any point on Earth and practically anything in orbit. However, we won't. The threat—plus the short-range weapons—should protect us from counterattack. We will sit tight, and thus realize our objective: to keep the blood of possibly millions off American hands, while giving America the self-determination that once was hers.")

Turn the Decaturists over to the Communists. Let all the ists kill each other off and leave human beings in peace.

("My friend, my friend," Mannix sighed, "you cannot be naïve enough to suppose the Asians have no hand in this. You yourself, I find, were involved in our rocket-scattering of munitions across the rebellious parts of India. Have they not been advising, subsidizing, equipping, infiltrating the upper leadership of your oh-so-patriotic Decatur Society? Let the Soviet Union ruin itself—which is the likeliest outcome if America doesn't intervene—let that happen, and yes, America could probably become the boss of the Western Hemisphere. But we're not equipped to conquer the Eastern. You're aware of that. The gooks would inherit. The Russians may gripe you. You may consider our native leaders their puppets. But at least they're white; at least they share a tradition with us. Why, they helped us back on our feet, Jim, after the war. They let us rearm, they aided it, precisely so we could cover each other's backs, they in the Old World, we in the

New. . . . Can you prove your Society isn't a Jappochink tool?")

No, but I can prove we have rockets here so we'll draw some of the Jappochink fire in the event of a big war. They're working on suicide regardless of what I do, Bonnie. America would already have declared for one splinter or the other, if America weren't likewise divided. Remember your Shakespeare? Well, Caesar has conquered the available world and is dead; Anthony and Octavian are disputing his loot. What paralyzes America is—has to be—a silent struggle in Washington. Maybe not altogether silent; I get word of troop movements, "military exercises" under separate commands, throughout the Atlantic states. . . . Where can we hide, Bonnie?

("We have reason to believe," said the political lecturer to us at assembly, "that the conflict was instigated, to a considerable degree at least, by *agents provocateurs* of the Asian deviationists, who spent the past twenty years or more posing as Soviet citizens and worming their way close to the top. With our whole hearts we trust the dispute can be settled peacefully. Failing that, gentlemen, your duty will be to strike as ordered by your government to end this war before irrevocable damage has been done the Motherland.")

There is no place to hide, Bonnie Brighteyes. Nor can we bravely join the side of the angels. There are no angels either.

("Yeah, sure, I've heard the same," said Jack, who belonged to my cell. "If we grab those bases and refuse to join this fight, peace'll have to be negotiated, lives and cultural treasures 'ull be spared, the balance of power 'ull be preserved, yeah, yeah. Think, man. What do you suppose Sotomayor and the rest really want?

Isn't it for the war to grow hot—incandescent? Never mind who tries the first strike! The Kuninists might, thinking they'd better take advantage of a U.S. junta fairly sympathetic to them before it's overthrown. Or the Vasilievists might, they being Party types who can't well afford a compromise. Either way, no matter who comes out on top, the Soviets overnight turn themselves into the junior member of our partnership. Then *we* tell *them* what to do for a change.")

Not that I am altogether cynical, Bonnie. I don't choose to believe we've brought Chuck and Joan into a world of wolves and jackals—when you've said you wish for a couple more children. No, I've simply changed my mind, simply had demonstrated to me that our best chance—mankind's best chance—lies with the legitimate government of the United States as established by the People's Constitutional Convention.

Next day Mannix turned me over to his interrogation specialists, who asked me more questions than I'd known I had answers for. A trankstim pill kept me alert but unemotional, as if I were operating myself by remote control.

Among other items, I showed them how a Decaturist who had access to the right equipment made contact with fellows elsewhere, whom he'd probably never met, or with higher-ups whom he definitely hadn't. The method had been considered by political-police technicians, but they'd failed to devise any means of coping.

Problem: How do you maintain a network of illicit communications?

In practice you mostly use the old-fashioned mail drop. It's unfeasible to read the entire mails. The authorities must settle for watching the correspondence of suspicious individuals and these may have ways of posting and collecting letters unobserved.

Yet sometimes you need to send a message fast. The telephone's no good, of course, since computers became able to monitor every conversation continuously. However, those same machines, or their cousins, can be your carriers.

Remember, we have millions of computers around these days, nationally interconnected. They do drudge work like record-keeping and billing; they operate automated plants; they calculate for governmental planners and R & D workers; they integrate organizations; they keep day-by-day track of each citizen, etc. Still more than in the case of the mails, the volume of data transmissions would swamp human overseers.

Given suitable codes, programmers and other technicians can send practically anything practically anywhere. The printout is just another string of numbers to those who can't read it. Once it has been read, the card is recycled and the electronic traces are wiped as per routine. That message leaves the office in a single skull.

Naturally, you save this capability for your highest-priority calls. I'd used it a few times, attracting no attention since my job on base frequently required me to prepare or receive top-secret calculations.

I couldn't give Mannix's men any code except the latest that had been given me. Every such message was recoded en route, according to self-changing programs buried deep down in the banks of the machines concerned. I could, though, put him in touch with somebody close to Sotomayor. Or, rather, I could put myself in touch.

What would happen thereafter was uncertain. We couldn't develop an exact plan. My directive was to do my best and if my best was good enough I'd be pardoned and rewarded.

I was rehearsed in my cover story till I was letter perfect, and given a few items like phone numbers to learn. Simulators and reinforcement techniques made this quick.

Perhaps my oath-brothers would cut my throat immediately, as a regrettable precaution. That didn't seem to matter. The drug left me no particular emotion except a desire to get the business done.

As a minimum, I was sure to be interrogated, strip-searched, encephalogrammed, X-rayed, checked for metal and radioactivity. Perhaps blood, saliva, urine, and spinal fluid would be sampled. Agents have used pharmaceuticals and implants for too many years.

Nevertheless Mannix's outfit had a weapon prepared for me. It was not one the Army had been told about. I wondered what else the political police labs were working on. I also wondered if various prominent men, who might have been awkward to denounce, had really died of strokes or heart attacks.

"I can't tell you details," said a technician. "With your education, you can figure out the general idea for yourself. It's a micro-version of the fission gun, enclosed in lead to baffle detectors. You squeeze—you'll be shown how—and the system opens; a radioactive substance bombards another material which releases neutrons which touch off the fissionable atoms in one of ten successive chambers."

Despite my chemical coolness, awe drew a whistle from me. Given the right isotopes, configurations, and shielding, critical mass gets down to grams and you can direct the energy through a minilaser. I'd known that. In this system, the lower limit must be milligrams; and the efficiency must approach 100 percent if you could operate it right out of your own body.

Still . . . "You do have components that'll register if I'm checked very closely," I said.

The technician grinned. "I doubt you will be, where we have in mind. They'll load you tomorrow morning."

Because I'd need practice in the weapon, I wasn't drugged then. I'd expected to be embarrassed. But when I entered an instrument-crammed concrete room after being unable to eat breakfast, I suddenly began shaking.

Two P.P. men I hadn't met before waited for me. One wore a lab coat, one a medic's tunic. My escort said, "Dowling," closed the door, and left me alone with them.

Lab Coat was thin, bald, and sourpussed. "Okay, peel down and let's get started," he snapped.

Medic, who was a fattish blond, laughed—giggled, I thought in a gust of wanting to kill him. "Short-arm inspection," he said.

Bonnie, I reminded myself, and dropped my clothes on a chair. Their eyes went to my crotch. Mine couldn't. I bit jaws and fists together and stared at the wall beyond them.

Medic sat down. "Over here," he ordered. I obeyed, stood before him, felt him finger what was left. "Ah," he chuckled. "Balls but no musket, eh?"

"Shut up, funny man," Lab Coat said and handed him a pair of calipers. I felt him measure the stump.

"They should've left more," Lab Coat complained. "At least two centimeters more."

"This glue could stick it straight onto his bellybutton," Medic said.

"Yeah, but the gadgets aren't rechargeable," Lab Coat retorted. "He'll go through four or five today before the final one and nothing but elastic collars holding 'em in place. What a clot of time I'll have fitting *them*." He shuffled over to a workbench and got busy.

"Take a look at your new tool," Medic invited me. "Generous, eh? Be the envy of the neighborhood. And what a jolt for your wife."

The wave was red, not black, and tasted of blood. I lunged, laid fingers around his throat, and bawled—I can't remember—maybe, "Be quiet, you filthy fairy, before I kill you."

He squealed, then gurgled. I shook him till his teeth rattled. Lab Coat came on the run. "Stop that!" he barked. "Stop or I'll call a guard."

I let go, sank down on the floor—its chill flowed into my buttocks, up my spine, out along my ribcage—and struggled not to weep.

"You bastard," Medic chattered. "I'm gonna file charges. I am."

"You are not. Another peep and I'll report you." Lab Coat hunkered beside me, laid an arm around my shoulder, and said, "I understand, Dowling. It was heroic of you to volunteer. You'll get the real thing back when you're finished. Never forget that."

Volunteer?

Laughter exploded. I whooped, I howled, I rolled around and beat my fists on the concrete; my muscles ached from laughing when finally I won back to silence.

After that, and a short rest, I was calm—cold, even—and functioned well. My aim improved fast, till I could hole the center circle at every shot.

"You've ten charges," Lab Coat reminded me. "No more. The beam being narrow, the head's your best target. If the apparatus gets detected after all, or if you're in Dutch for some other reason and your ammo won't last, press inward from the end—like this—and it'll self-destruct. You'll be blown apart and escape a bad time. Understand? Repeat."

He didn't bother bidding me good-bye at the end of the session. (Medic was too sulky for words.) No doubt he'd figured what sympathy to administer earlier. Efficiency is the P.P. ideal. Mannix, or somebody, must have ordered my gun prepared almost at the moment I was arrested, or likelier before.

My escort had waited, stolid, throughout those hours. Though I recognized it was a practical matter of security, I felt hand-lickingly grateful to Mannix that this fellow—that very few people—knew what I was.

The day after, I placed my call to the Decaturists. It was brief. I had news of supreme importance—the fact I'd vanished for almost a month made this plausible—and would stand by for transportation at such-and-such different rendezvous, such-and-such different times.

Just before the first of these, I swallowed a stim with a hint of trank, in one of those capsules which attach to the stomach wall and spend the next hundred hours dissolving. No one expected I'd need more time before the metabolic price had to be paid. A blood test would show its presence, but if I was carrying a vital message, would I not have sneaked me a supercharger?

I was not met, and went back to my room and waited. A side effect, when every cell worked at peak, was longing for Bonnie. Nothing sentimental; I loved her, I wanted her, I had to keep thrusting away memories of eyes, lips, breasts beneath my hand till my hand traveled downward. . . . In the course of hours, I learned how to be a machine.

They came for me at the second spot on my list, a trifle past midnight. The place was a bar in a village of shops and rec centers near the base. It wasn't the sleek, state-owned New West, where I'd be recognized by officers, engineers, and Party functionaries who could afford to patronize. This was a dim and dingy shack, run by a couple of workers on their own time, at the tough end of town. Music, mostly dirty songs, blared from a taper, ear-hurtingly loud, and the booze was rotgut served in glasses which seldom got washed. Nevertheless I had to push through the crowd and, practically, the smoke—pot as well as tobacco. The air also smelled of sweat and urine.

You see more of this kind of thing every year. I imagine the government only deplores the trend officially. People need some unorganized pleasure. Or, as the old joke goes, "What is the stage between socialism and communism called? Alcoholism."

A girl in a skimpy dress made me a business offer. She wasn't bad-looking, in a sleazy fashion, and last month, I'd merely have said no, thanks. As was, the drug in me didn't stop me from screaming, "Get away, you whore." Scared, she backed off, and I drew looks from the men around. In cheap civies, I was supposed to be inconspicuous. Jim Dowling, officer, rocketeer, triple agent, boy wonder, ha! I elbowed my way onward to the bar. Two quick shots eased my shakes and the crowd around forgot me.

I'd almost decided to leave when a finger tapped my arm. A completely forgettable little man stood there. "Excuse me," he said. "Aren't you Sam Chalmers?"

"Uh, no, I'm his brother Roy." Beneath the once more cold surface, my pulse knocked harder.

"Well, well," he said. "Your father's told me a lot

about you both. My name's Ralph Wagner."

"Yes, he's mentioned you. Glad to meet you, Comrade Wagner."

We shook hands and ad-libbed conversation a while. The counter-signs we'd used were doubtless obsolete, but he'd allowed for my having been out of touch. Presently we left.

A car bearing Department of Security insignia was perched on the curb. Two much larger men, uniformed, waited inside. We joined them, the blowers whirred, and we were off. One man touched a button. A steel plate slid down and cut us three in the rear seat off from the driver. The windows I could see turned opaque. I had no need to know where we were bound. I did estimate our acceleration and thus our cruising speed. About three hundred K.P.H. Going some, even for a security vehicle!

From what Granddad had told me, this would have been lunacy before the war. Automobiles were so thick then that often they could barely crawl along. Among my earliest memories is that the government was still congratulating itself on having solved that problem.

Wind hooted around the shell. A slight vibration thrummed through my bones. The overhead light was singularly bleak. The big man on my left and the small man on my right crowded me.

"Okay," said the big man, "what happened?"

"I'll handle this," said he who named himself Wagner. The bruiser snapped his mouth shut and settled back. He was probably the one who'd kill me if that was deemed needful, but he was not the boss.

"We've been alarmed about you." Wagner spoke as gently as Mannix. In an acid way I liked the fact that he didn't smile.

I attempted humor in my loneliness: "I'd be alarmed if you hadn't been."

"Well?"

"I was called in for top-secret conferences. They've flitted me in and out—to Europe and back—under maximum security."

The big man formed an oath. Wagner waited.

"They've gotten wind of our project," I said.

"I don't know of any other vanishments than yours," Wagner answered, flat-voiced.

"Would you?" I challenged.

He shrugged. "Perhaps not."

"Actually," I continued, "I wasn't told about arrests and there may have been none. What they discussed was the Society, the Asians—they have a fixed idea the Peking-Tokyo Axis has taken over the Society—and what they called 'open indications.' The legal or semilegal talk you hear about 'socialist lawfulness,' 'American socialism,' and the rest. Roger Mannix—he turns out to be high in the P.P., by the way, and a shrewd man; I recommend we try to knock him off—Mannix takes these signs more seriously than I'd imagined anybody in the government did." I cleared my throat. "Details at your convenience. The upshot is, the authorities decided there is a definite risk of a cabal seizing the rocket bases. Never mind whether they have the data to make that a completely logical conclusion. What counts is that it *is* their conclusion."

"And right, Goddamn it, right," muttered the big man. He slammed a fist on his knee.

"What do they propose to do?" Wagner asked, as if I'd revealed the government was considering a reduced egg ration.

"That was a . . . tough question." I stared at the

blank, enclosing panel. "They dare not shut down the installations, under guard of P.P. who don't know a mass ratio from a hole in the ground. Nor dare they purge the personnel, hoping to be left with loyal skeleton crews—because they aren't yet sure who those crews had better be loyal to. Oh, I saw generals and commissioners scuttling around like toads in a chamberpot, believe me." Now I turned my head to confront his eyes. "And believe me," I added, "we were lucky they happened to include one Decatur man."

Again, under the tranquilization and the stimulation (how keenly I saw the wrinkles around his mouth, heard cleft air brawl, felt the shiver of speed, snuffed stale bodies, registered the prickle of hairs and sweat glands, the tightened belly muscles and self-seizing guts beneath!), fear fluttered in me, and under the fear I was hollow. The man on whom I had turned my back could put a gun muzzle at the base of my skull.

Wagner nodded. "Yes-s-s."

Though it was not too early to allow myself relief, I saw I'd passed the first watchdog. The Society might have been keeping such close survelliance that Wagner would know there had in fact been no mysterious travels of assorted missilemen.

This wasn't plausible, Mannix had declared. The Society was limited in what it could do. Watching every nonmember's every movement was ridiculous.

"Have they reached a decision?" Wagner asked.

"Yes." No matter how level I tried to keep it, my voice seemed to shiver the bones in my head. "American personnel will be replaced by foreigners till the crisis is past. I suppose you know West Europe has a good many competent rocketeers. In civilian jobs, of course; still, they could handle a military assignment.

And they'd be docile, regardless of who gave orders. The Spanish and French especially, considering how the purges went through those countries. In short, they'd not be players in the game, just parts of the machinery."

My whetted ears heard him let out a breath. "When?"

"Not certain. A move of that kind needs study and planning beforehand. A couple—three weeks? My word is that we'd better compress our own timetable."

"Indeed. Indeed." Wagner bayoneted me with his stare. "If you are correct."

"You mean if I'm telling the truth," I said on his behalf.

"You understand, Colonel Dowling, you'll have to be quizzed and examined. And we'll meet an ironic obstacle in your conditioning against involuntary betrayal of secrets."

"Eventually you'd better go ahead and trust me . . . after all these years."

"I think that will be decided on the top level."

They took me to a well-equipped room somewhere and put me through the works. They were no more unkind than necessary, but extremely thorough. Never mind details of those ten or fifteen hours. The thoroughness was not quite sufficient. My immunity and my story held up. The physical checks showed nothing suspicious. Mannix had said, "I expect an inhibition too deep for consciousness will prevent the idea from occurring to them." I'd agreed. The reality was what had overrun me.

Afterward I was given a meal and—since I'd freely admitted being full of stim—some hours under a sleep inducer. It didn't prevent dreams which I still shiver to recall. But when I was allowed to wake, I felt rested and ready for action.

Whether I'd get any was an interesting question. Mannix's hope was that I'd be taken to see persons high in the outfit, from whom I might obtain information on plans and membership. But maybe I'd be sent straight home. My yarn declared that, after the bout of talks was over, I'd requested a few days' leave, hinting to my superiors that I had a girl friend out of town.

My guards, two young men now grown affable, couldn't guess what the outcome would be. We started a poker game, but eventually found ourselves talking. These were full-time undergrounders. I asked what made them abandon their original identities. The first said, "Oh, I got caught strewing pamphlets and had to run. What brought me into the Society to start with was . . . well, one damn thing after another, like when I was a miner and they boosted our quota too high for us to maintain safety structures and a cave-in killed a buddy of mine."

The second, more bookish, said thoughtfully: "I believe in God."

I raised my brows. "Really? Well, you're not forbidden to go to church. You might not get a good job, positively never a clearance, but—"

"That's not the point. I've heard a lot of preachers in a lot of different places. They're all wind-up toys of the state. The Social Gospel, you know—no, I guess you don't."

Wagner arrived soon afterward. His surface calm was like Dacron crackling in a wind. "Word's come, Dowling," he announced. "They want to interview you, ask your opinions, your impressions, you having been our sole man on the spot."

I rose. "They?"

"The main leadership. Sotomayor himself, and his chief administrators. Here." Wagner handed me a wallet. "Your new I.D. card, travel permit, ration tab, the works, including a couple of family snapshots. Learn it. We leave in an hour."

I scarcely heard the latter part. Alfredo Sotomayor! The half-legendary president of the whole Society!

I'd wondered plenty about him. Little was known. His face was a fixture on post-office walls, wanted for a variety of capital crimes, armed and dangerous. The text barely hinted at his political significance. Evidently the government didn't wish to arouse curiosity. The story told me, while I was in the long process of joining, was that he'd been a firebrand in his youth, an icily brilliant organizer in middle life, and in his old age was a scholar and philosopher, at work on a proposal for establishing a "free country," whatever that meant. Interested, I'd asked for some of his writings. They were denied me. Possession was dangerous. Why risk a useful man unnecessarily?

I was to meet rebellious Lucifer.

Whom once I had served. Whom I would be serving yet had not the political police laid hand on me and mine.

Not that those fingers had closed on Bonnie or the kids. They would if I didn't undo my own rebelliousness. Camp La Pasionara. What was Sotomayor to me?

How could I believe a bandit had any real interest in America, except to plunder her? I had *not* been shown those writings.

"You feel well, Jim?" asked the man who believed in God. "You look kind of pale."

"Yeah, I'm okay," I mumbled. "Better sit down, though, and learn my new name."

A fake security car, windows blanked, could bring me to an expendable hidey-hole like this, off in a lonely section of hills. The method was too showy for a meeting which included brains, heart, and maybe spinal cord of Decatur. Wagner and I would use public transportation.

We walked to the nearest depot, a few kilometers off. I'd have enjoyed the sunlight, woods, peace asparkle with birdsong, if Bonnie had been my companion (and I whole, I whole). As was, neither of us spoke. At the newsstand I bought a magazine and read about official plans for my future while the train was an hour late. It lost another hour, for some unexplained reason, en route. About par for the course. Several times the coach rattled to the sonic booms of military jets. Again, nothing unusual, especially in times of crisis. The People's Republic keeps abundant warcraft.

Our destination was Oakland. We arrived at 2000, when the factories were letting out, and joined the pedestrian swarm. I don't like city dwellers. They smell sour and look grubby. Well, that's not their fault; if soap and hot water are in short supply, people crowded together will not be clean. But their grayness goes deeper than their skins—except in ethnic districts, of course, which hold more life but which you'd better visit in armed groups.

Wagner and I found a restaurant and made the conversation of two petty production managers on a business trip. I flatter myself that I gave a good performance. Concentration on it took my mind off the food and service.

Afterward we saw a movie, an insipidity about boy volunteer on vacation meets girl on collective. When it and the political reel had been endured, meeting time was upon us. We hadn't been stopped to show our papers, and surely any plainclothesman running a random surveillance had lost interest in us. A streetcar groaned us to a surprisingly swank part of town; and the house to which we walked was a big old mansion in big old grounds full of the night breath of roses.

"Isn't this too conspicuous?" I wondered.

"Ever tried being inconspicuous in a tenement?" Wagner responded. "The poor may hate the civil police, but the prospect of reward money makes them eyes and ears for the P.P."

He hesitated. "Since you could check it out later anyway," he said, "I may as well tell you we're at the home of Lorenzo Berg, commissioner of electric power for Northern California. He's been one of us since his national-service days."

I barely maintained my steady pace. This fact alone would buy me back my life.

A prominent man is a watched man. Berg's task in the Society had been to build, over the years, the image of a competent bureaucrat who had no further ambitions and therefore was no potential menace to anybody, but who amused himself by throwing little parties where screwball intellectuals would gather to discuss the theory of chess or the origin of Australopithecus. Most of these affairs were genuine. For the few that weren't, he had the craft to nullify the bugs in his house and later play tapes for them which had been supplied him. Of course, a mobile tapper could have registered what was actually said—he dared not screen the place—but the P.P. had more to do than make anything but spot checks on a harmless eccentric.

Thus Berg could provide a scene for occasional important Society meetings. He could temporarily shelter fugitives. He could maintain for this area that vastly

underrated tool—a reference library; who'd look past
the covers of his many books and microreels? Doubtless
his services went further, but never into foolish flam-
boyancies.

I don't recall him except as a blur. He played his
role that well, even that night among those men. Or
was it his role? You needn't be a burning-eyed vision-
ary to live by a cause.

A couple like that were on hand. They must have
been able in their fields. But one spoke of his specialty,
massive sabotage, too lovingly for me. My missiles were
counterforce weapons, not botulin mists released among
women and children. Another, who was a black, dwelt
on Russian racism. I'm sure his citations were accurate,
of how the composition of the Politburo has never since
the beginning reflected the nationalities in the Soviet
Union. Yet what had that to do with us and why did
his eyes dwell so broodingly on the whites in the room?

The remaining half dozen were entirely businesslike
in their various ways, except Sotomayor, who gave me
a courteous greeting and then sat quietly and listened.
They were ordinary Americans, which is to say a mixed
lot: a second black man, a Jew to judge by the nose (it
flitted across my mind how our schools keep teaching
that the People's Republic has abolished the prejudices
of the imperialist era, which are described in detail),
a Japanese-descended woman, the rest of them like
me . . . except, again, Sotomayor, who I think was almost pure Indio. His features were rather long and lean
for that, but he had the cheekbones, the enduringly
healthy brown skin, dark eyes altogether alive under
straight white hair, flared nostrils, and a sensitive
mouth. He dressed elegantly, and sat and stood as erect
as a burning candle.

I repeated my story, was asked intelligent questions,

and carried everything off well. Maybe I was helped by Bonnie having told me a lot about theater and persuading me to take occasional bit parts. The hours ticked by. Finally, around 0100, Sotomayor stirred and said in his soft but youthful voice: "Gentlemen, I think perhaps we have done enough for the present, and it might arouse curiosity if the living-room lights shone very late on a midweek night. Please think about this matter as carefully as it deserves. You will be notified as to time and place of our next meeting."

All but one being from out of town, they would sleep here. Berg led them off to their cots. Sotomayor said he would guide me. Smiling, as we started up a grand staircase the Socialist Functionalist critics would never allow to be built today, he took my arm and suggested a nightcap.

He rated a suite cleared for his use.

Although a widower, Berg maintained a large household. Four grown sons pleaded the apartment shortage as a reason for living here with their families and so preventing the mansion's conversion to an ordinary tenement. They and the wives the Society had chosen for them had long since been instructed to stay completely passive, except for keeping their kids from overhearing anything, and to know nothing of Society affairs.

Given that population under this roof, plus a habit of inviting visiting colleagues to bunk with him, plus always offering overnight accommodations when parties got wet, Berg found that guests of his drew no undue notice.

All in all, I'd entered quite a nest. And the king hornet was bowing me through his door.

The room around me was softly lit, well furnished,

dominated by books and a picture window. The latter overlooked a sweep of city—lanes of street lamps cut through humpbacked darknesses of buildings—and the Bay and a deeper spark-speckled shadow which was San Francisco. A nearly full moon bridged the waters with frailty. I wondered if men would ever get back yonder. The requirements of defense against the revisionists—

Why in the name of madness was I thinking about that?

Sotomayor closed the door and went to a table whereon stood a bottle, a carafe of water, and an ice bucket which must be an heirloom. "Please be seated, Colonel Dowling," he said. "I have only this to offer you, but it is genuinely from Scotland. You need a drink, I'm sure, tense as you are."

"D-does it show that much?" Hearing the idiocy of the question, I hauled myself to full awareness. Tomorrow morning, when the group dispersed, Wagner would conduct me home and I would report to Mannix. My job was to stay alive until then.

"No surprise." He busied himself. "In fact, your conduct has been remarkable throughout. I'm grateful for more than your service, tremendous though that may turn out to be. I'm joyful to know we have a man like you. The kind is rare and precious."

I sat down and told myself over and over that he was my enemy. "You, uh, you overrate me, sir."

"No. I have been in this business too long to cherish illusions. Men are limited creatures at best. This may perhaps make their striving correspondingly more noble, but the limitations remain. When a strong, sharp tool comes to hand, we cherish it."

He handed me my drink, took a chair opposite me, and sipped at his own. I could barely meet those eyes, however gentle they seemed. Mine stung. I took a long gulp and blurted the first words that it occurred to me might stave off silence: "Why, when being in the Society is such a risk, sir, would anybody join who's not, well, unusual?"

"Yes, in certain cases, through force of circumstance. We have taken in criminals—murderers, thieves— when they looked potentially useful."

After a moment of stillness, he added slowly: "In fact, revolutionaries, be they Decaturists or members of other outfits or isolated in their private angers— revolutionaries have always had motivations as various as their humanity. Some are idealists; yet let us admit that some of the ideals are nasty, like racism or religious fanaticism. Some want revenge for harm done them or theirs by officials who may have been sadistic or corrupt, but often were merely incompetent or over-zealous in a system which allows the citizen no appeal. Some hope for money or power or fame under a new dispensation. Some are old-fashioned patriots who want us out of the empire. Am I right that you fall in that category, Colonel Dowling?"

"Yes," I said, you were.

Sotomayor's gaze went into me and beyond me, across city and waters, skyward. "One reason I want to know you better," he said, "is that I think you can be educated to a higher ideal."

I discovered, with a sort of happiness, that I was interested enough to take my mind off the fact I was drinking the liquor of a man who believed I was his friend and a man. "To your own purposes, sir?" I asked. "You know, I never have been told what you yourself are after."

"On as motley a collection as our members are, the effect of an official doctrine would be disruptive. Nor is any required. The history of communist movements in the last century gives ample proof. I've dug into history, you realize. The franker material is hard to find, after periodic purges of the libraries. But it's difficult to eliminate a book totally. The printing press is a more powerful weapon than any gun—for us or for our masters." Sotomayor smiled and sighed. "I ramble. Getting old. Still, I have spent these last years of mine trying to understand what we are doing in the hope we can do what is right."

"And what are your conclusions, sir?"

"Let us imagine our takeover plan succeeds," he answered. "We hold the rocket bases. Given those, I assure you there are enough members and sympathizers in the rest of the armed services and in civilian life that, while there will doubtless be some shooting, the government will topple and we will take over the nation."

The drink slopped in my hand. Sweat prickled forth on my skin and ran down my ribs.

Sotomayor nodded. "Yes, we are that far along," he said. "After many years and many human sacrifices, we are finally prepared. The war has given us the opportunity to use what we built."

Surely, I thought, wildly, the P.P., military intelligence, high Party officials, surely they knew something of the sort was in the wind. You can't altogether conceal a trend of such magnitude.

Evidently they did not suspect how far along it was.

Or . . . wait . . . You didn't need an enormous number of would-be rebels in the officer corps. You really only needed access to the dossiers and psychographs kept on everybody. Then in-depth studies would give you a good notion of how the different key men would react.

"Let us assume, then, a junta," Sotomayor was saying. "It cannot, must not, be for more than the duration of the emergency. Civilian government must be restored and made firm. But *what* government? That is the problem I have been working on."

"And?" I responded in my daze.

"Have you ever read the original Constitution of the United States? The one drawn in Philadelphia in 1787?"

"Why . . . well, no. What for?"

"It may be found in scholarly works. A document so widely disseminated cannot be gotten rid of in thirty or forty years. Though if the present system endures, I do not give the old Constitution another fifty." Sotomayor leaned forward. Beneath his softness, intensity mounted. "What were you taught about it in school?"

"Oh . . . well, uh, let me think . . . Codification of the law for the bourgeoisie of the cities and the slaveowners of the South . . . Modified as capitalism evolved into imperialism . . . "

"Read it sometime." A thin finger pointed at a shelf. "Take it to bed with you. It's quite brief."

After a moment: "Its history is long, though, Colonel Dowling, and complicated, and not always pleasant—especially toward the end, when the original concept had largely been lost sight of. Yet it was the most profoundly revolutionary thing set down on paper since the New Testament."

"Huh?"

He smiled again. "Read it, I say, and compare today's version, and look up certain thinkers who are mentioned in footnotes if at all—Hobbes, Locke, Hamilton, Burke, and the rest. Then do your own thinking. That won't be easy. Some of the finest minds which ever existed spent centuries groping toward the idea that law should be a contract the people make among each other, and that every man has absolute rights, which protect him in making his private destiny and may never be taken from him."

His smile had dissolved. I have seldom heard a bleaker tone: "Think how radical that is. Too radical, perhaps. The world found it easier to bring back overlords, compulsory belief, and neolithic god-kings."

"W-would you ... revive the old government?"

"Not precisely. The country and its people are too changed from what they were. I think, however, we could bring back Jefferson's original idea. We could write a basic law which does not compromise with the state, and hope that in time the people will again understand."

He had spoken as if at a sacrament. Abruptly he shook himself, laughed a little, and raised his glass. "Well!" he said. "You didn't come here for a lecture. *A vuestra salud.*"

My hand still shook when I drank with him.

"We'd better discuss your personal plans," he suggested. "I know you've had a hatful of business lately, but none of us dare stay longer than overnight here. Where might you like to go?"

"Sir?" I didn't grasp his meaning at once. Drug or no, my brain was turning slowly under its burdens. "Why ... home. Back to base. Where else?"

"Oh, no. Can't be. I said you have proved you are not a man we want to risk."

"Bu-but ... if I don't go back, it's a giveaway!"

"No fears. We have experts at this sort of thing. You will be provided unquestionable reasons why your leave should be extended. A nervous collapse, maybe, plausible in view of the recent strains on you, and fake-able to fool any military medic into prescribing a rest cure. Why, your family can probably join you at some pleasant spot." Sotomayor chuckled. "Oh, you'll work hard. We want you in consultation, and between times I want to educate you. We'll try to arrange a suitable replacement at Reed. But one missile base is actually less important than the duties I have in mind for you."

I dropped my glass. The room whirled. Through a blur I saw Sotomayor jump up and bend over me, heard his voice: "What's the matter? Are you sick?"

Yes, I was. From a blow to the . . . the belly.

I rallied, and knew I might argue for being returned home, and knew it would be no use. Fending off his anxious hands, I got to my feet. "Exhaustion, I guess," I slurred. "Be okay in a minute. Which way's, uh, bathroom?"

"Here." He took my arm again.

When the door had closed on him, I stood in tiled sterility and confronted my face. But adrenalin pumped through me; and Mannix's chemicals were still there Everything Mannix had done was still there.

If I stalled until too late . . . the Lomonosov Institute might or might not survive. If it did, I might or might not be admitted. If it didn't, something equivalent might or might not be built elsewhere in some latter year. I might or might not get the benefit thereof, before I was too old.

Meanwhile Bonnie—and my duty was not, not to anybody's vague dream—and I had barely a minute to decide—and it would take longer than that to change my most recent programming—

Act! yelled the chemicals.

I zipped down my pants, took my gun in my right hand, and opened the door.

Sotomayor had waited outside. At his back I saw the main room, water, moon, stars. Astonishment smashed his dignity. "Dowling, *¿está Usted loco?* What the flaming hell—?"

Each word I spoke made me more sure, more efficient: "This is a weapon. Stand back."

Instead, he approached. I remembered he had been in single combats and remained vigorous and leathery. I aimed past him and squeezed as I had been taught. The flash of light burned a hole through the carpet and floorboards at his feet. Smoke spurted from the pockmark. It smelled harsh.

Sotomayor halted, knees bent, hands cocked. Once, hunting in the piny woods of my boyhood, we'd cornered a bobcat. It had stood the way he did, teeth peeled but body crouched motionless, watching every instant for a chance to break free.

I nodded. "Yeah," I said. "A zap gun. Sorry, I've changed teams."

He didn't stir, didn't speak, until he forced me to add: "Back. To yonder phone I see. I've got a call to make." My lips twitched sideways. "I can't very well do otherwise, can I?"

"Has that thing—" he whispered, "has that thing been substituted for the original?"

"Yes," I said. "Forget your *machismo.* I've got the glands."

"Pugilist," he breathed, almost wonderingly.

Faintly through the blood-filled stiffness of me, I felt surprise. "What?"

"The ancient Romans often did the same to their pugilists," he said in a monotone. "Slaves who boxed in the arenas, iron on their fists. The man kept his physical strength, you see, but his bitterness made him fight without fear or pity.... Yes. Pavlov and those who used Pavlov's discoveries frequently get good reconditioning results from castration. Such a fundamental shock. This is more efficient. Yes."

Fury leaped in me. "Shut your mouth. They'll grow me back what I've lost. I love my wife."

Sotomayor shook his head. "Love is a convenient instrument for the almighty state, no?"

He had no right to look that scornful, like some aristocrat. History has dismissed them, the damned feudal oppressors; and when the men in this house were seized, and the information in its files, his own castle would crash down.

He made a move. I leveled my weapon. His right hand simply gestured, touching brow, lips, breast, left and right shoulders. "Move!" I ordered.

He did—straight at me, shouting loud enough to wake the dead in Philadelphia.

I fired into his mouth. His head disintegrated. A cooked eyeball rolled out. But he had such speed that his corpse knocked me over.

I tore free of the embrace of those arms, spat out his blood, and leaped to lock the hall door. Knocking began a minute afterward, and the dry, "What's wrong? Let me in!"

"Everything's all right," I told the panel. "Comrade Sotomayor slipped and nearly fell. I caught him."

"Why's he silent? Let us in."

I'd expected nothing different, and was already dragging furniture in front of the door. Blows and kicks, clamor and curses waxed beyond. I scuttled to the telephone—sure, they provided this headquarters well—and punched the number Mannix had given me. An impulse would go directly to a computer which would trace the line and dispatch an emergency squad here. Five minutes?

They threw themselves at the door, thud, thud, thud. That isn't as easy as the movies pretend. It would go down before long, though. I used bed, chairs, and tables to barricade the bathroom door. I chinked my fortress with books and placed myself behind, leaving a loophole.

When they burst through, I shot and I shot and I shot. I grew hoarse from yelling. The air grew sharp with ozone and thick with cooked meat.

Two dead, several wounded, the attackers retreated. It had dawned on them that I must have summoned help and they'd better get out.

The choppers descended as they reached the street.

My rescuers of the civil police hadn't been told anything, merely given a Condition A order to raid a place. So I must be held with the other survivors to wait for higher authority. Since the matter was obviously important, this house was the jail which would preserve the most discretion.

But they had no reason to doubt my statement that I was a political agent. I'd better be confined respectfully. The captain offered me my pick of rooms, and was surprised when I asked for Sotomayor's if the mess there had been cleaned up.

Among other features, it was the farthest away from everybody else, the farthest above the land.

Also, it had that bottle. I could drink if not sleep. When that didn't lift my post-combat sadness, I started thumbing through books. There was nothing else to do in the night silence.

I read: "We hold these Truths to be self-evident, that

all Men are created equal, that they are endowed by their Creator with certain inalienable Rights, that among these are Life, Liberty, and the Pursuit of Happiness—That to secure these Rights, Governments are instituted among Men, deriving their just Powers from the Consent of the Governed, that whenever any Form of Government becomes destructive of those Ends, it is the Right of the People to alter or to abolish it, and to institute a new Government, laying its Foundation on such Principles, and organizing its Powers in such Form, as to them shall seem most likely to effect their Safety and Happiness."

I read: "We the people of the United States . . . secure the blessings of liberty to ourselves and our posterity . . ."

I read: "Congress shall make no law respecting an establishment of religion, or prohibiting the free exercise thereof; or abridging the freedom of speech, or of the press; or the right of the people peacefully to assemble, and to petition the Government for a redress of grievances."

I read: "The powers not delegated to the United States by the Constitution, nor prohibited by it to the States, are reserved to the States respectively, or to the people."

I read: "I have sworn upon the altar of God eternal hostility toward every form of tyranny over the mind of man."

I read: "In giving freedom to the slave, we assure freedom to the free—honourable alike in what we give and what we preserve."

I read: "But they shall sit every man under his vine and under his fig tree; and none shall make them afraid. . . ."

When Mannix arrived—in person—he blamed my sobbing on sheer weariness. He may have been right.

Oh, yes, he kept his promise. My part in this affair could not be completely shielded from suspicion among what rebels escaped the roundup. A marked man, I had my best chance in transferring to the technical branch of the political police. They reward good service.

So, after our internal crisis was over and the threat of our rockets made the Kunin faction quit, with gratifyingly little damage done the Motherland: I went to Moscow and returned whole

Only it's no good with Bonnie, I'm no good at all.

When Poul wrote this, it wasn't fashionable to think of Communists as real enemies. That was all hysteria.

I've heard that proposition defended on many an American university campus by students and faculty alike.

Strangely enough, though, I haven't heard many Cambodians, or Czechs, or Hungarians, or Poles say it. . . . And now we hear from Afghanistan. . . .

Like me, Anderson has other visions of the future; he too can see a path to peace, liberty, and freedom. But it takes work, and we are not at the moment working.

I began including poetry in anthologies quite by accident: that is, I found one piece irresistible for Black Holes *(Fawcett) and that led to including a couple more; then when I did my next, I invited all previous contributors to submit work, and in came poetry I thought worth publishing. By now it's a tradition. I also find myself the major publisher of SF poetry, which shows just how little is being published. . . .*

I've never met Peter Dillingham, but he has contributed to four of my anthologies now. Thus I wrote to ask him for some biographical data.

He sent the following:

"Peter Dillingham is a science-fiction writer who prefers to work in poetry rather than prose."

Informative, isn't it?

holovision/20-20

by peter dillingham

Wave-length (meters)		Frequency (hertz)
1.2×10^{-9}	A bracelet of bright diffraction Fleurets about the carpus, So lovely long and graceful, Like bamboo shoots, those phalanges, Demurely hiding all but her orbits	2.5×10^{17}
1.5×10^{-7}	Behind a Spring bouquet Of yellow treacle mustard, Rape petals' muted purple, And crimson charlock. Then briefly, O so briefly,	2×10^{15}
4×10^{-7}	The bloom of flesh unfolds, The rainbow hues of eyes and hair And lips and cheeks, Wreathed in yellow blossoms... A radiant vision too swiftly vanished,	7.5×10^{14}
2×10^{-6}	Banished by a blush's stark white flower.	1.5×10^{14}

Dian Girard is a lovely svelte brunette (usually; the hair color changes like dreams. I'd swear it once was blue). Her principal character is a dippy twenty-first century lady who just manages to cope with the world of 2020.

Actually, Cheryl copes quite well; one sometimes thinks it's the world that's not ready for Cheryl. But this was one of the first Cheryl Harbottle stories, of a time before she became so well adjusted to the Good Life.

The real-world Dian has been known to act a bit like Cheryl herself; but it's all an act. The real Dian is a supervisor in a large computer firm, and her husband is a computer engineer/designer. It's just possible that she's been peeking over his shoulder and has seen a real vision of the future, one that Chuck is even now inventing.

If so, we can hope that for the good of us all she'll strangle him one fine night.

eat, drink, and be merry

by dian girard

The gentle purr of the alarm brought her out of a half-remembered dream into the soft gray of morning. A muttered "murmpf!" next to her indicated Logan was at least awake, and Cheryl yawned deliciously as the wall lighting came up to a warm and toasty gold.

"Toasty. Oh, I wish I hadn't though of that," she mused hungrily. "Well, maybe today will be the day."

A gentle kick with both feet propelled her backsliding spouse into new wakefulness. Mock resentful, he nibbled at her right ear. "Up," she said. "Up, up, up!"

"Murmpf." Cheryl slid out of bed and padded softly to the bathroom. The ambient temperature of the room was already a good deal warmer than when she had first awakened, and she wondered idly what the temperature was like three stories above in the open air. She paused at the door to check the intercom into the boys' room and the sounds of a healthy—and very loud—argument over ownership of a sweatshirt assured her they were awake.

She turned to consider the shower. "Maybe, just maybe," she muttered, "maybe I could step around it. Or not take a shower at all." She rejected this last as unworkable. Once and only once she'd made that attempt, only to find the bathroom door locked and a gently chiding mechanical voice saying "Mrs. Harbottle, we've neglected our personal hygiene this morning, haven't we?" Ugh.

She bent to gaze in wrinkle-browed concentration at the large black square on the shower floor. The tubular matrix of the shower stall reached from floor to ceiling and was about four and a half feet in diameter. The black square touched the inside wall at four corners and its nonskid surface stared at her complacently.

A protesting howl from the bedroom told her that, having had its refrigerator coils ignored, the bed had now administered the first of its electrical shocks. Her tousle-haired husband came into the room looking a trifle wary. "Should have got up when I did!" she gloated.

He slapped her lightly on the fanny and headed for the shower.

"Honey!" she yelped, catching him in midstride. "Let's take a shower together, hmmmm?"

"You nuts or sump'n?"

Cheryl put on her very best pout. "People used to take showers together, all sort of snuggly and warm, and I could wash your back or something like that."

"The needle spray does all that, and besides we could never get in there together. There isn't room."

"Sure there is. I'll get in first and sort of scrunch over against the side while you get in."

"Okay, kook. Scrunch if it makes you happy." He kissed her on the nose.

Cheryl stepped into the shower, carefully avoiding the black area and leaning against the far wall with her feet uncomfortably on either side of one black angle, resting her weight mostly on one leg. She moved the other foot to touch the black surface lightly, biting her lower lip in concentration. She watched Logan's right foot as he stepped through the door, and as he stepped down she quickly shifted her weight.

She sighed happily and put her arms around his waist as he slid the door shut. The shower had compensated for his height instead of hers and she got a mouthful of soapsuds, but what the hell, you can't have everything.

Wash, rinse, and warm-air dry. Logan slid the door open and stepped out before she had a chance to yelp Oh, blast.

Chestnut curls drooping forlornly, Cheryl stared down at her feet planted firmly in the middle of the black square. She sighed.

When she walked into the dining room, neatly attired in a nonorganic Marsfluf robe with gold frogs, her husband was pulling the first page of the morning paper out of the sender, and the boys were still fighting over the sweatshirt. That there were four more in the drawer didn't seem to matter at all.

"Bob," she said firmly, "you sit over here where you can't fight with your brother."

They both looked at her, mouths agape. They'd been sitting in the same places for as long as either could remember.

"No arguments," she snapped, her heart beating furiously and her hopes rising seventeen points. Bob, who was eight, moved over to his mother's chair and Cheryl sat in his—or pretented to sit as she supported most of her weight above it. "You can dial breakfast, too," she said.

This treat removed all objections and he rapidly coded in eggs, bacon, pancakes, and orange juice under the envious eyes of his six-year-old brother. With a flourish he added coffee for his parents and two glasses of milk.

Within two minutes the table panels began to slide back. The trays rose from the bowels of the robot chef. Cheryl, her heart in her mouth and her ankles giving out under the strain, watched with dreadful anticipation as the tray rose toward her. Bob was already busily downing his pancakes and eggs in her usual seat.

The tray stopped and clicked into place.

One half grapefruit. One piece of dry toast. One cup of coffee—black. She felt like crying. She did cry. Also, she let her 132 pounds settle into the chair. The computer had figured it all out anyway.

Two pounds, she thought bitterly. Two lousy pounds. She nibbled at her toast. She'd always hated toast. Dry toast, anyway.

She resented her husband. There he sat, callously consuming thick succulent pancakes, dripping with mouth-watering maple-flavored syrup and golden butter substitute. He even used the final moist, flavorful bite to dab up the last deep yellow drops of vitamin-fortified low-cholesterol egg yolk. He crammed the slices of bacon into his unfeeling, bestial face, washing them down with coffee and not even pausing to savor the Hickory Smoked Goodness, or the Delectable Crunchy Texture.

Fleeting, satisfying, heartwarming visions of divorce flickered through her tortured head. Freedom, and charming beaux, their features invisible but every detail of their presents plain, her visions included: men with Bonbons. Whitman's Sampler. MacDonald's MacDonaldburgers, yet, for God's sake! Fried Chicken. Pizza. More candy.

She didn't even consider the fate of her orphaned

children. She could tell they were unfeeling brutes, true sons of a bestial father, by the very way they guzzled their fresh, vitamin-enriched, golden-yellow flavor-fortified orange juice.

Ten minutes later, Bob and Teddy were on the way to school and Logan had been straightened, face-wiped, kissed, and sent off to work. Cheryl watched the table ingest the breakfast plates, puttered around a little, and craftily decided to do her hair and go shopping.

"Logan needs new shirts," she said loudly. "I want to pick them myself. And the boys could use some underwear, and I need a checkup." The machine never answered, but it was watching her. She knew, she knew. She very carefully wrote down all the things she would buy.

But inside, where the machine couldn't see, she watched with rapture: snack shops, coffee shops, tearooms, sandwich bars. Her mind gloated.

Duly machine-coiffed and wearing her newest spring suit, Cheryl took the tube car to the first level, where natural sunlight streamed down through translucent panels into the controlled environment. Trees, grass, and flowers grew in the middle of the Mall just as they did under the artificial sunlight on fourth level, but here popular music replaced the recorded Bird Calls and Rustling Leaves of all residential areas. Cheryl browsed contentedly, making all the purchases she had in mind, buying a few knicknacks besides, and always working her way stealthily toward the Kopper Kornukopia Koffee Korner in the middle of the block.

At eleven-thirty she settled gratefully into a booth, slipped off her shoes, and punched her credit card into the proper slot. A moment of delicious anticipation, and then the serious business of ordering lunch.

She lingered enjoyably over the menu card, and finally dialed a chocolate malt, french fries, a Denver sandwich, and cherry pie ala mode.

The Café-Serv beeped quietly as if in reproach. A suave metallic voice—it seemed to fit well into the Kopper Kornukopia Koffee Korner in the middle of the block—said softly, "Your order exceeds your allowable dietary intake for this day by 2,575 calories, Mrs. Harbottle. Please reorder."

Savagely she punched the Dieter's Special. The wall panel opened and dispensed her tray. One meat patty, small, a scoop of cottage cheese, three tomato slices on a withered lettuce leaf, and a cup of tea. No sugar. Cheryl ate glumly.

Like a starved explorer of some bygone era, she paused craftily outside the café and looked up and down the street. Two blocks away the French Chocolate Shop leered at her like the wicked witch. With an apple. With a whole gingerbread house. Which she could eat in one sitting. Cheryl stalked her prey determinedly, her mind racing furiously.

Like most stores, there were no clerks. Mouth-watering assortments of candies were temptingly displayed behind lucite panels. All the adjectival art of the best copysmiths had gone into making the legends on the brass placques below an adventure in starvation just to be read. Sales machines stood shiningly in the center of the room.

Cheryl chose vanilla cremes at $2.65 a pound, punched for store delivery, inserted her card, and waited expectantly.

This machine had an accented contralto. "Sorree, madame, but we cannot deliver luxury calorics to zomeone on caloric limitation. May we hold the order for eventual deliveree?"

"But it's a gift."

"Sorree, madame...."

Cheryl punched the CANCEL button and dragged wearily out of the shop. Conspiracy, she thought. And all for two lousy pounds. She felt as if the entire computer intertie system was designed just to thwart her, personally.

A tear stole down Cheryl's cheek. The cashless society had eliminated small change, too. She couldn't even buy that slightly used lollypop from the gluttonous happy-faced kid who wandered past.

The next shop wouldn't even deliver a pizza to her neighbor. As a gift.

Feeling sorry for herself and in a mood to eat five pounds of chocolate divinity with pecans if only to spite the General Health Coordination Plan, she descended a level to the General Services area. Medical checkups were a bore, but every citizen was required to have one twice a year. Besides, she hadn't been feeling well lately. "Probably undernourished," she muttered savagely.

Two hours later she stepped back into the apartment, noting that her morning purchases—minus chocolates—had been delivered. She'd have to start thinking about what to dial for dinner pretty soon. Dinner for Logan and the boys. She knew all too well what *her* dinner would be ...

Maybe, she thought hopefully, just maybe I've walked enough to lose the two pounds. She went into the bathroom, stripped, and stepped onto the black square in the shower. Standing firmly—there wasn't any point in trying to settle part of her weight on the stall structure, she'd found—she touched the eye-level square marked VISUAL.

A small dark square lit up 125 in green. Beneath it,

a red 132.5 shone like a death sentence. Two and five tenths above the allowable five-pound deviation above or below optimum weight. No dinner tonight, none at all. No nice fluffy dinner rolls, no crêpes for appetizers, no mousse for dessert, no baked potato—an infinite list of "no's" loomed endlessly before her, stretched out in fantastic array, all the forbidden delights across a vast Sahara of food.

Thinking soulfully of Danish pastry, she dressed in a flowing hostess gown, did her hair in a softer style, and waited for her family to come home. The boys were first, at 4:35, then Logan at 5:03. Washed, combed, and hungry, her men settled to the table while Cheryl began to dial dinner, wondering mournfully what sort of Dieter's Joy she'd get in lieu of the Beef Stroganoff, Egg Noodles with Poppy Seeds, and Chocolate Torte.

The delivery slot across the hall dispensed an orange envelope from Health Services. Bob retrieved it for her as she finished coding in a cucumber-and-tomato salad.

She opened the letter, read it, and passed it wordlessly to her husband. Her eyes glistened with joyful anticipation. Her tray rose laden with succulent dishes, and the machine's voice noted: "Maternity situations necessitate increased consumption of calcium, Mrs. Harbottle. High Calcium Food has been added to your dessert selection."

Cheryl blissfully dipped a spoon into the vanilla ice cream next to her chocolate torte. "Nyah!" she screamed at the machine. "Nyah, nyah, nyah!"

David McDaniel was a good storyteller who wrote far too little before he died young in a home accident. He was a good friend, and I'm damned if I'm going to let a story introduction become an obituary. Instead I'll excerpt from the introduction I used in the first edition:

Dave McDaniel is a careful young man who truly gets absorbed into what he's writing at the moment. When he was working on novelizations of the Man from U.N.C.L.E. *series, he accumulated a bewildering array of U.N.C.L.E. fountain pens, guns, communicators, badges, heat rays, and other gadgets. He had badges identifying himself as an agent of both U.N.C.L.E. and the archvillainous T.H.R.U.S.H.*

He even made himself a model of the personal computer terminal which figures so largely in this story. He carried it with him at all times to get practice using it, startling casual passersby; not that that bothered him. Dave was once an organizer of the Institute for Temporal Research, a group of bright young fanatics who—well, it's hard to describe what they did. Example: they would go to a crowded bus terminal and look around, staring at everyone; one would take out a very futuristically wrapped candy bar and begin eating, dropping the wrapper on the floor; whereupon the tour leader would

*come over and point at it and make the miscreant pick
it up—and also* put back on the floor *the perfectly ordinary gum wrapper he'd tried to sneak into his pocket.
In fact, they so perfectly imitated a team of time travelers
studying the twentieth century (and determined to
change nothing, of course) that they had a local TV
station director wondering just who was putting whom
on; after all, wouldn't that be a perfect disguise for* real
time travelers?

*This story is the most traditional in the book, and
comes closest to what I had in mind when I dreamed
up this anthology. It has details of a real and tangible
future, a wealthy and happy one, which we could get to
from here. Of course wealth and general happiness don't
eliminate all personal problems.*

prognosis: terminal

by david mcdaniel

It would seem insensitive to commit suicide on such a nice day. Great masses of clouds piled white on gray in the eastern sky and late-afternoon sunlight shafted bright orange through the western wall of the dome between dark glassy towers. That wall should have been polarized by this hour but wasn't, and Buzz Hoffer squinted into the glare ahead as the westbound Olympic pedway carried him out of the subterranean dimness of the South BevHills corridor into the vast open space under Century Dome.

Everyone else shielded their eyes to stare down into the small Pubscreen at each seat; Buzz felt a self-conscious contempt for them as he twisted to look back over his shoulder and saw a distant iceberg of piercing white cumulus above the gray billowing clouds which had raised the local watertable a fraction of an inch in the last ten hours. The ozone-count in the dome was up, which may also have helped, but contemplation of the celestial vista seemed to cheer him faintly.

He'd half-planned to ride the pedway to Santa Monica and drown himself near the old pier later this evening, but, once having admitted the serene beauty spreading across the sky, the thought of personal dissolution became gradually more abstract. After all, he wasn't in any hurry. . . .

Impulsively he punched off at Fox Boulevard and moments later stepped from the open car to a braking platform along with a few other socially blank-faced passengers, most of whom shifted to the northbound lane without breaking stride. Not even Buzz stopped to watch two men fighting in the pit area to one side; their short capes draped over the side bench were left undisturbed as they slugged and grappled and panted over some personal dispute which was nobody else's business.

The pedway interchange floated on wide graceful struts above a tiled plaza where people sat or wandered among fountains and flowers, and forty flashing pubscreens on short pillars displayed every free channel to a largely oblivious audience.

Buzz believed he thought better on his feet, and he felt enough proprietary interest in this unnoticed sunset to want to see it unfiltered. Hillcrest Park was half a mile away, just beyond the south edge of the dome, and foot traffic on the mall was light. He fed fifty cents to a dispenser for a shot of Kalm and strolled south, sucking idly on the lime-green tube.

After all, Lars or Penta might call with confirmation of their Nabe company. If this weekend gig could really come off, they would all eat well and maybe meet some important people. But with the defection of their hastily recruited empath most of his hope had faded. They seemed doomed to fall back on the dole.

This was the prospect that had started him toward the harbor an hour earlier. Standing in line for free artificial food, living in barracks on ten ikes a day—it took half that just to pay storage on his mass while he was doling.

As he walked, the curtain speech from *Chisara* came back to him, recalling the noble grace with which he had played that classic suicide, and the lines echoed in his mind to the rhythm of his stride. *"And when at last inexorable Fate / Brings force from every side to show his mastery, / Then must a man of firm resolve rise up / And prove by deed that human will, indomitable, / Can burst the straitened bonds of flesh and shake the dice anew."*

His phone chirped over the last two bars; he fished it out, flipped it open, and fitted it to his ear. "If it's not money or a girl," he said, "cut off."

"Sorry—I don't satisfy either."

"Hyo, Lars. What's the bad news?"

"You've got it—a total null. Barclay canceled the entire gig. His group voted to go for a linked Lysamine drop with alpha-stim instead."

"And flash their troubles away, huh? That cheap sensationalist! I always had a feeling he'd fade under pressure—ever since we found out he ran a Tarky stand in Burbank Dome. I knew right then, in the pit of my stomach, it just wasn't going to run. He's cheap! He's got no taste, no imagination, no—"

"He takes half a meg a year out of that Tarky stand. They sell sushi and piroshki, and the whole Insnak catalog, not to mention every soft high on the market. He could afford to stage a live production if he wanted to. But he's all the way into this Sharing Group, and he isn't going to push for us if they decide they want linked Lysamine instead of a genuine experience."

"But they *know* it's not real. Way down inside, Lysamine or not, they know before they start it won't be real, and they'll know afterwards it wasn't real, even if they do all remember the same thing. What ever happened to nonparticipant audiences?"

"They watch holo all day."

"But our whole Nabe is going to come apart," Buzz

said. "We can't let that happen. We've got to keep working together."

"We've all got other things to do. Roger's got a buyer for his *Cacaphonic Variations* tape, Doc's preparing for the Hyperdip compugame semifinals next month, Penta has her ethnic analysis project.... We'll all stay in touch, and if something turns up we can wire in together again."

"Maybe we could set up a stage in a park." Buzz carried his conversation to a vacant bench and sat down, ignoring the Pubscreen which muttered above his head. "We could do scenes, and people would pay us."

"That hasn't been practical for fifty years. Where do you think we are—feudal Europe? You'd only draw a pack of haijin who'd sooner watch a fight. You can try it if you want; I'm going to punch Central Library and sign up for another Reference contract."

"I'd almost rather ride the dole than go back to refaiding. Sitting for hours with your phone connected to an endless parade of incredibly dull people who aren't even sure what it is they can't find? At least when you're doling your time's your own."

"Refaide pays twenty dollars an hour—punch on for five hours and your residence system is grounded for another week. Two or three hours a day would be all you'd need, if you worked Fridays. That extra day grounds my terminal charge. And I want to get back to work on my scanimated abstract visualization of Tepper's *Fantasia on a Theme of Paganini for Tympani and Piano.* I couldn't do that doling. My privacy is worth too much."

"The pigeonhole I'm filed in isn't worth half the hundred ikes I'm paying anyway. But fifteen hours a week as the human factor in Refsection is too much."

"Then go dole," said Lars, dismissing the subject.

"But don't program-stash any of your mass with me, because I'm cramped now."

"I have a reputable agency," Buzz retorted, stung, since that very thought had just crossed his mind. "If I'm forced to fold in, they'll handle everything."

"You've been there before," said Lars. "Well, let me know what you decide. Gotta cut. Sayonara."

"Sayonara."

The western wall of the dome had polarized during the conversation, and Buzz could now look directly into fat ruddy sun. One of the upper pedestrian bridges between buildings opposite carried tiny gliding forms like a scalloped ribbon of black paper directly across the center of the fiery disc.

He finished his Kalm, then crunched up the sticky ascorbic collagen tube. As he did he thought Penta might not have heard about the final cancellation. He punched her two-digit code and listened to the circuitry replay her number. A moment later she answered.

"Hyo?"

"Hyo, Penta. Have you heard from Lars?"

"About Barclay shorting out? I was on the line when he did. Well, that's show business," she said sympathetically. "What'll you do now?"

"I was thinking about taking the Nabe out in a park, without any production support at all, and doing live scenes with a few people. But Lars seemed pretty sure it wouldn't work."

"He's probably right. Besides, hardly anybody would want to join you in the risk. Better you should go back to refaiding."

"Lars said that too. He thinks the living stage went out a hundred years ago."

"With film, TV and holo, who needed it, except for snob appeal?"

"That's what I mean. At least a hundred years ago

we weren't competing with everybody else in the world. You only had to be the best Nabe in town. I wish to Sine there was something I could do that fifteen million other people weren't doing!"

"Oh, stop it, Buzz! Nobody else in the world can create a character or turn a line exactly like you. All you have to do is find an audience capable of appreciating you. Esthetic sense can always be sold, because more people can appreciate it than have it. You have it."

"I wish enough people could appreciate it to give it a commercial premium."

"*Proxy Paradise* was miles ahead of anything Dikki has done, and look where he is now. If you could've gotten that into a Festival...."

"Nobody wins Festivals but amateurs with faddish flash, who do what the Festival wants. I wish I could have an audience all to myself."

"Raw ego. Competition stiffens you up—makes you work harder. Besides, it's naturalaw. You just don't believe in yourself. Have you tried Di-Beta therapy?"

"You and your fads. Next thing I know you'll have your teeth tinted."

"And the front two jeweled. You never saw such a dazzling smile."

"I'm on my pocket phone, remember? I'll punch you back when I get home and see it."

"Oh, switch over! I'm only stoning you. I wouldn't really do that—it looks gaudy. I just thought I'd shake your frame a little."

"Leave my frame alone. It's bent up enough the way the world's been coming down on me. The whole Nabe is coming apart. You and Lars and the rest don't need it now; Roger hasn't been comfortable working with me since he blew that scene in *TARTUFFE* and I overloaded on him afterwards; Dikki doesn't even know me any more since he struck it rich and moved to Baja—"

"You know better than that; he probably hasn't had time, since he's just finished polishing his second set of casets for I.F.A. His first set went so well he renegotiated, got a quarter percent more, and Eden was passed for another pregnancy. So he's been working doubletime since they got their estate. Eden called me Tuesday after lunch, which is how I know all this; she showed me around their place. It's huge! Eight or nine rooms, with a couple of private cans, and literally *acres* of open ground around the house. They're just back from the bay on the first mound, and there's a hydro that runs up and down the coast every hour. It's only ninety minutes from San Pedro. But Dikki does all his work through his terminal. Eden says the whole town is wired for them, and I.F.A. *gave* him a Cineborg 1708 to play with. He does everything through it, direct to their banks here in L.A. Anyway, Eden invited me down. Why don't you call Dikki this evening and make a little rap? If you can coax an invitation out of him, I'll go with you."

"Rap on what? The minute he sees me he'll think I just want to make a touch. Everybody else who knew him here will be after him for something—I'll just be lost in the crowd again. I wish I could get away from all the other people who want what I want. I wish there was some kind of small-time left. There's no more little-theater or club circuits; even the Nabes are dying. Everything local is done by part-time amateurs who work for nothing; everything on the screens is done by a couple thousand people, with a million more talented hopefuls trying to cut themselves in. There's no place any more for a merely competent actor or writer or director to start and build something of his own."

"How dedicated you are? Doling isn't any worse than starving in a garret—most ways it's better. Go back to the locals and form a new Nabe. Work for nothing. You should be willing to suffer for your art."

"Flux!" Buzz swore. "Where would I go from the Nabes anyway? Unless I do something really outstanding, something that'll get me noticed, I'll be stuck there for the rest of my life and leave nothing solid of my work behind but a few audio tracks and a file full of hardcopy. And that's a scrawny sort of immortality. At least a hundred years ago you could travel from town to town with one good show and peddle it for years without ever repeating audiences. And since they didn't watch Darlo Green on holo every week, they appreciated what they got. Now everybody already knows everything. They've already seen everything, and there's nothing I can show them that they haven't seen better."

"Fifty years ago somebody was lamenting that there were no more suckers. But I saw a bit on the news just last month about a woman in Barstow buying a money-printing machine. Oh, that reminds me—not to change the subject—there was something else I saw I thought you might be interested in. Did you hear about the exsolar signal?"

"Huh?"

"Even the popnews channels carried it when it started a couple of weeks ago. That thirty-year-old radiotelescope in Mare Moscovienses picked it up first, and they got the cleanest take."

"You're stoning me again. I never heard a thing about it."

"Well, punch in. There's probably a lot I don't know about it, but they think it's connected with a nova about a quarter of the way around the galaxy."

"A signal? You mean something intelligent from a nova?"

"They think so."

"How?"

"I doubt if anybody within a few thousand light-years knows. The first signals, I think they said, were the numbers from one to eight, in plain unmodulated pulses, and then a few progressions and some number concepts all came through, repeated a lot, for the first few days. Then two days ago I heard it had stopped, but the computers were still analysing most of it. I left a newscan memo keyed to *exsolar* and *nova,* and today there are six essays available at a quarter-ike. You could probably catch one on Pubscreen if you scanned the programming."

The magnitude of the concept dawned slowly in Buzz's consciousness. "Real alien intelligence!" he said. "Another race! I wonder what they're like. I wonder what they'll tell us. Maybe they know the secret of faster-than-light travel. If we had a million colonies scattered around on different planets, there'd be enough new worlds to conquer for everybody! You could start with a colony and found your own school of theater. Have a World Art Center named after you in a few generations."

"You don't want much."

"I'd be willing to devote the rest of my life to it."

"Hot out! How long do you think it would take to start a million colonies? Or even a thousand? Even if they started next week, and especially if there is any way around the Einstein barrier, which still doesn't look likely, how long do you expect to wait? Or can you afford to be frozen?"

"I was thinking about a long sleep just this afternoon," Buzz said coldly. "But I put it off to watch a sunset which is just now beginning. Can you see west from where you are?"

"Yeah—as far as the wall."

"Forget it. Look, I'll think about talking to Dikki in the next few days if I can think of something to tell him besides my financial problems. Would you like to have dinner with me tonight?"

"Can't, Buzz. I'm doing a number."

"With Roger?"

"Jealous?"

"Yes."

"No."

"No?"

"No, not with Roger," she said. "It's a six-hour meditation trip, and I've already dropped. It'll be coming on in another few minutes, so I'll be closing my phone. Tomorrow night?"

"I'll meet you at Shrdlu."

"At seventeen hundred. Sayonara."

"Sayonara, Penta."

Buzz folded his phone and rose from the bench. The wide mall was not crowded, and he resumed his stroll toward the park. Fifteen feet above him soared the silent pedway, passengers slipping along three times as fast as he walked, their shadows flickering across the glazed face of Kinney Tower to his left beyond a green pond of grass dotted with islets of flowers. On every supporting pylon six shimmering pubscreens faced two or three rows of oblivious benches, their muted speakers supplying a continuous gentle babble like water on rocks; an amplified audio track was instantly available on any pocketphone. He ignored them, pacing south, thinking.

What might this exsolar signal mean? Would it be

a message of deliverance for the race of men? Would it be gibberish? Could we tell the difference?

He was still chewing it over when he passed through the air curtain at Pico and ducked through a short tunnel to emerge in the park. Here it was cooler, and even the sinking sun radiated only a reminder of warmth. Hillside trees and distant towers were gilded with sprays of light through a scattered rack of clouds like a cheap inspirational holo. The sky overhead was patched with shaggy strips and tufts of golden fleece across shifting holes of deep infinite blue slipping east away from the sun, after the rain.

Too much of his mind was occupied by speculation on this incredible signal from infinitely remote intelligence. Determined to free his thoughts for appreciation of the sunset immediately before him, he sat down on the grass, leaned against a convenient tree, and opened his phone again. Three digits gave him Pubscreen Log and he keyed *"Exsolar."*

His phone spoke. "Essay by William Caldiron on cultural implications of exsolar signal, twenty minutes; paid cast at 1800 on channel 32 *(pip)*. Metagogical analysis of exsolar Tau factor by Segart Dowell, sixty minutes; paid cast at 2130 on channel 19 *(pip)*. Precis of translated exsolar signal prepared by I-S-C, twenty minutes; paid cast tomorrow 13 March at 1600 on channel 28 *(pip)*. Full transcript of exsolar signal is available in hardcopy for five dollars by punching 400-391-7402-99 *(beep)*."

Caldiron's essay came on in fifteen minutes; that would probably tell him as much as he could understand. Buzz set his reminder, put the phone away, and got up nervously, looking around for people. Under distant trees blue-brown nitelites were already coming on, leaving only the illusion of darkness where the ruddy light of the sun did not reach. After grokking the unchanging sunset for another minute or two, Buzz turned and wandered up the gentle slope toward the dispenser pavilion at the crest.

It wasn't particularly crowded—a pack of haijin clustered around a Sniper game at the far side of the transplex geodesic, yelling obscenities and side bets as play progressed.

He fed another half-ike into a slot for a two-pack of Tingles while a freckled, rugged boyish face on the screen above his head said in synthesized sincerity, "The *Eagle* was a good little ship—but if I was going to the Moon today, I'd go by *Transpace*, the luxury line!" Buzz popped one into his mouth to suck and dropped the other in his pouch as irate voices raised behind him penetrated the social barrier.

"Fade that, stud!" someone snapped; Buzz's curiosity got the better of his conditioning and he turned to look. The command had been thrown at the taller of two young men, who was eying a slender, frightened girl who clung to her light-bearded protector, author of the brusque order. Another girl shrank back against the display wall.

The object of the warning, restrained by his anxious companion, sneered, "Why should I—when you have two and we don't have any?"

"Stop it, Kenny," urged the shorter. "What do you want them for? We've got each other."

"She's been giving me the nod—haven't you, cunny?" She didn't answer, and he shifted angry-eyed focus to her protector. "I don't think you're enough stud to keep two foxes; I don't even think you can keep one."

The subject of their controversy did not participate, but withdrew to join the other girl as the aggressor stepped forward. Their stud was quick in their defense;

a swift punch-kick threw him back into the arms of his friend, who shrieked in shared agony. "Kenny! Are you hurt?"

Kenny shook his head, recovering his breath and balance, as the other hurled himself, shrieking vengeance, at the bearded man. Both girls retreated along the wall as a doubled attack carried their champion to the ground. A moment later Kenny rose to advance on his spoils, one of whom objected unexpectedly.

"Get away from me, you fung, or I'll scream monitor!"

The second attacker seemed less interested in the girls than in the dazed form of their fallen stud. Experimentally he kicked him in the side as the girls began to scream. Buzz looked around. The haijin pack had stopped playing to watch; nobody else seemed to notice.

Suddenly angered at the victor's unsocial behavior and spurred by the fact that he was crouching to jump with both feet on his fallen opponent, Buzz sprinted past five people and slammed the little bully in the small of the back just as he leaped, knocking him into a sprawling tangle of arms and legs which tumbled howling across the floor to fetch up against a pubscreen pedestal. Somehow a dozen people managed to move out of his way without ever noticing him.

Kenny turned from the girls toward Buzz, focused, and lunged as the other scrambled to his feet, livid with rage, and charged back into the fray to be met by the man whose rib cage Buzz had saved, now rising to defend himself.

A moment later half-a-dozen haijin, unable to resist the diversion, joined the brawl with savage yells, and the disinterested bystanders suddenly vacated the area. Three seconds after that jets high on the pedestal sprayed a pink cloud which swiftly filled the immediate area as air curtains switched on to confine it. But Buzz didn't see them—like everyone else in the fight he had fallen asleep.

He was quite comfortable when he woke up in a living chair, its gentle massage soothing his sore arm. The wall facing him was pale green, and the aide who handed him a cup of something refreshing wore a soft yellow suit.

"Are you feeling all right, Mr. Hoffer?" she asked.

"Oh . . . I guess so. What happened?"

"The stud that set it off was busted; the others were let off with a warning. The tapes showed you to be innocent of first- or second-degree aggression, so we just wanted to apologize for gassing you and hope that it hasn't caused any inconvenience."

"What time is it?"

"Eighteen-oh-five. Can we help you get somewhere?"

"No, nothing important." He sipped the sparkling euphoric and gathered himself. "The last I noticed was a mob of haijin coming in. Was that what set things off?"

"Yes. With more than eight people involved, riot regs cut in."

"Lucky for me it was all taped. Did that fox actually give him the nod?"

"Sorry, I'm not allowed to discuss pending cases."

"Sorry I asked." Buzz finished his drink as the chair switched off. "If there's nothing else then . . ."

She helped him to his feet. "Nice to have had you as a guest, sir."

The escalator brought him to the surface facing the remains of a spectacular sunset. Above the kiosk blue-brown nightlites were on, illuminating without dispelling the deep shadows beneath the sheltering trees. As he came from under the arching branches the sky spread out before him, from the hot core of molten gold beyond Westwood Dome and the Santa Monica mountains ascending through cooling layers and bands of orange and misty red. The thinning patches of cloud which still passed leisurely eastward were now a darkening rose against eternal purple, with one bright planet shining like a star above the sunken solar glow.

This reminded him of the exsolar cast, and he looked around for a pubscreen display as he got out his phone to punch the audio channel. His message light glowed; he ignored it, hurrying across the twilit grass toward the central pavilion where crowds of people moved about under dancing lights among pubscreens and holo displays.

He slipped the privacy plug in his ear as he approached and found a voice saying, ". . . have not been able to guess the method used to modulate the gigawatts of energy behind this signal. Faced by their outrushing doom, trapped on their planet by the immutable laws of the universe, they may have found some way of tapping a tiny fraction of the vast and cataclysmic outburst from their traitor sun; an installation on an outer planet might have lasted as long as this signal, the death cry of a race so much like our in so many ways. I'll discuss the significance of these facts and their implications for our own future after this local pitch."

"Hyo, friends, Ralph Williams Three here from our big display center in Bel-Aire where we have every type of house module ready for custom installation—"

Buzz cut the audio to concentrate on moving through

the milling mob inside the airy geodesic toward the screen labled 32, where images of luxuriously furnished rooms succeeded one another hypnotically interspersed with a flashing phone number.

The message light still glowed on his phone; with one eye on the pubscreen he punched playback and heard an unfamiliar voice say, "Hyo—we couldn't loiter til we got out, but me and my sister wanna do something to thank you for saving us this afternoon—and that feeble stud, too. Punch me at 468-2103-72 anytime after twenty hundred and I'll thank you in person. By the way, my name's Jam."

The voice sounded promising; Buzz replayed the number and copied it into bank, then left a reminder for 2030. By this time the rooms on the pubscreen had been replaced by a smiling, talking face and Buzz punched back to audio 32.

". . . serving Greater L.A. for three-quarters of a century. Now back to this fine free essay, brought to you as a public service by Ralph Williams Three, the best man to see for all your housing needs."

William Caldiron returned to the screen, and his already-familiar voice filled the right half of Buzz's head.

"Much of the final part of the signal remains to be analyzed. Some of it may never be understood. But one thing is terribly plain—one fact stares us in the face, hollow eye-sockets leering at us with grim inevitability. This distant, dead race, with the technology and audacity to tap the very energy of the nova which destroyed their system, were not able to break the Einsteinian bonds which held them as surely as they hold us prisoners in our own solar system; the same inexorable laws which delayed even the light of their funeral pyre thirty thousand years."

Caldiron displayed a mane of white hair and a noble brow, both probably dubbed into his image. He was a littly hammy, Buzz thought, but he might say more about the aliens. There wasn't to be any star drive after all!

"Now, our sun isn't going nova for a long time. But the human race has always been exploring, spreading, reaching beyond what was known to seek out all the secrets of the universe. A hundred years ago we covered this little planet, and mastered its whims and ways; in the last fifty years we have sprung to the planets. The Moon is nearer than Siberia was a century past; in two years the Mars base will become a minimally self-sustaining colony. But neither there nor on Venus, even if the pilot dome there proves viable, will we find a new world truly hospitable to our human bodies.

"Nearly every star of the same type as our sun gives birth to planets, and every system seems to contain one or two where you could run around barefoot. But unless generations of pilgrims man gigantic colony ships on century-long voyages or the cold-sleep is perfected and automated, there will be no more frontiers. Either way, there could be no more communication with the departed pioneers than with the dead; it would be centuries before we could even know if they had arrived safely.

"So it appears we are all passengers in the same cosmic boat to infinity. There is no place else for us to go. After a quarter of a million years of climbing mountains, fording rivers, crossing oceans and going down into them to find out what is there, this restless inquisitive monkey-thing, *Man*, has come to the end of the unknown. He has reached his limit, covered his little ball of rock from pole to pole, and met himself coming back around the other side. While all the rest of this vast unexplored universe waits, enticing, just too far away for mortal hands to grasp—all we can do is look at it.

"Maybe it's better this way. Mankind has mastered his home planet and all its contents—except himself. The great riddles of good and evil, life and death, love and hate, remain unanswered. Maybe we shouldn't venture to other planetary systems for a while; at least not until we have a clearer understanding of what we are doing, have done, and should do. The laws of the universe seem to say, don't start bothering your neighbors before you know who *you* really are. Perhaps Man cannot explore the stars before exploring his own soul."

An anonymous elbow caught Buzz painfully in the short ribs and knocked his attention askew. When he recovered his balance, glaring around angrily, the shifting crowd had swallowed the offender. Oblivious, Caldiron continued. He seemed to be leading up to something.

"For as long as we know, Man has been running off in one direction or another in search of new fields. Now all directions have led back to the middle, and this dynamic, insatiably curious super-monkey, having suddenly overrun his island planet, has reached the end of his range. Now at last he must sit down and look at himself. And talk to himself about it.

"For the last several years, and with increasing efficiency, nearly every individual on earth has had the technological capability of finding out anything that was known, talking to anyone else in the world, communicating to large numbers and listening to others. Like synapses in a gigantic world-brain, we are infinitely interconnected.

"For the next thousand years, or five hundred, or ten thousand years, we will be talking to ourselves—

about everything. With ten billion individuals all wired together, some tremendous things could happen; the human brain has only about ten billion cells, and most of them aren't working all the time either. The human race itself is approaching a comparable systemic complexity, and miracles are likely to happen.

"Until they do, this lonely monkey with a conscience will have to sit here on his rock, through unguessable ages, riding around and around his incubator star—endlessly talking to himself. The only hope is that eventually he will work out some of the answers, and then with developing spiritual maturity he will be ready to leave his Terrestrial nest behind. This is William Caldiron; thank you for listening."

"Hyo, friends. This free cast was paid for by Ralph Williams Three, who assumes neither responsibility nor control for its contents. Copies may be ordered through our order phone for twenty-five cents, or come on down to our big display center in Bel-Aire—"

Buzz punched off and looked around for an opening in the crowd, through which he fought his way toward open air. Caldiron's style was awfully florid, and his metaphors didn't always hold together; as a reasonably representative sample of the kind of man Caldiron referred to, hopes for a new world of his own evaporated, Buzz felt anything but lonely. Jostled on every side by the press of oblivious bodies, breathing the exhalations of strangers, he felt numbly aware of the ten billion monkeys who shared this little ball of rock.

Ten billion monkeys on a rock. It had a nice swing to it. *Twenty billion monkeys on a rock* sounded even better, and there would probably be that many before long. *Twenty billion monkeys on a rock!* A dance number? A song? Why, he could build an entire show around that theme, with the rhythm as a bridge between segments showing the infinitely interconnected race of man, strung together in a chain of communication through an everyman plot. . . .

He stood glassy-eyed near the edge of the crowd, his back against a dispenser bank, blind to the world as the possibilities for effective live or holo staging of developments on this theme cascaded across his mind. Concepts exploded through his consciousness in swift tumultuous clarity, blending, shaping, suggesting sequences, effects, bits of action and design, touches of color, lighting, and composition—whole pattern structures formed themselves in seconds around his rhythmically stated theme before someone backed into him and came down on his right foot with blind weight.

He yelped as the owner of the weight jumped back and started a formal apology. Buzz was rude to him and stalked off, groping among sundered synapses for shards of that flash of inspiration. The basic line and overall concept were still there, and as he limped angrily away from the pavilion into the deepening twilight several fragments bearing recognizable ideas floated near the surface of his mind.

As he sorted through them, a corner of his thoughts turned to Dikki and the possibility of punching him up to pitch this new idea while it was fresh in his creative imagination. An unoccupied tree stump—charred, carven and hacked—gave him a place to sit while he punched Baja directory. The phone number was entered directly into his personal bank; he punched 2-48 to retrieve and apply it. A second later the accomplished connection was followed by the regular chirp of the ringing signal.

"Dikki Delongpre," answered a familiar voice. "Who's there?"

"Buzz Hoffer. Penta said you might have some free time now, and I thought I'd punch in and see."

"Hyo, Buzz! Glad you called. But I wish you'd punched on holo; I've got a new toy I want to show off if you have a few minutes. Are you near a public booth?"

"Yeah, but I can't really afford..."

"I'll ground the charge. Just give me the code and I'll punch right back."

"Okay. I'm out in Hillcrest Park, but there's a couple booths not far away. I'm going there now. What I really wanted to do was discuss a show I just had an idea for. Have you heard about the exsolar signal?"

"From the nova in Aquila? Just a little. Didn't it stop again after just a couple of weeks?"

"That's what I heard. Penta put me onto a free cast of an essay about it. I missed most of it, but the part I heard gave me the idea for this show I want to talk to you about."

"What kind of show?"

"More like a review, really. I got the theme from something the essayer said, but it's not close enough to infringe. I don't even have a presentation yet; I just thought of it about five minutes ago. Here's the booth. Ready to record? 213-475-2802-00, standing by."

He punched off, closed the door of the private cubicle, and settled himself in the middle chair. One touch on the arm panel opaqued all but the far wall, which grew transparent and began to glow like radon fog. Buzz touched the answer tab and soft light came up to surround him.

The fog he faced swirled into a scrambled rainbow and dissolved, revealing Dikki standing in what appeared to be the main room of a Roman villa, opening on a balcony which looked down past Mediterranean pines to an impossibly blue sea. The decor was even more remarkable, including polished marble columns as thick as trees, fantastic furs draped about the floor and furniture, and three unidentifiable and unclad girls lounging in the middle distance. Most remarkable of all was Dikki himself, taller, looking healthier and somehow handsomer than Buzz remembered him. He wore a properly folded Roman toga, and a laurel wreath at a rakish angle.

Buzz stared, while Dikki grinned. At last he said, "You're looking awfully well after only two months out of the city."

Dikki laughed delightedly. "You have no idea," he said. "How do you like the layout? Look pretty good?" He turned and walked a few steps toward the balcony, pausing by a pillar. "It ought to—I spent enough time on it." He did something out of sight on the pillar, and the room vanished.

Dikki stood in the same position, now wearing a tigerskin and longer hair, his hand resting on a fat stalagmite. Beyond him a vast arching cavern glittered with native gems. He turned back to Buzz. "See what I mean?"

Buzz found his breath again. "This is your Cineborg?" he asked.

Dikki nodded. "I haven't begun to find out all the things I can do with it. But here's one. . . ."

Without a flicker or a blink, Dikki was replaced by a three-foot gnome with green skin and warts, who jumped up and down comically and swung its arms. "Look," it said in a voice like rusted armor. "Almost any degree of direct image modulation, and a bank of secondary and tertiary holo modulators with a twelve-buss insert generator and independant scanimation faders." The grotesque creature fingered the stalagmite again and said, "This was the first one I tried."

Dikki stood, in shirt, shorts and sandals, on the surface of the Moon. Not far away the dome of Tranquility Park threw blinding sunlight back at them, and the Earth hung fat and marbled fifteen degrees above the near horizon. Dikki looked more like his old self, too, if tanner. "Watch my hand, now," he said. "If I do this right...."

He bent down and scooped up a handful of dark-gray soil. Some trickled between his fingers as he compacted it and tossed the loose ball toward the dome in the distance. It made a slow graceful parabola and dust spurted where it hit. "I put the Earth down there because it looked better."

"You've got your own image modifier off now, right?" said Buzz.

"Oh, right. But I've got to show you—now where is that control box?" Dikki groped about him for a moment, then connected. They stood in the main hall of a Norman castle, with men-at-arms stationed beneath shield-punctuated tapestries and flaring torches. Distant footsteps echoed on stone. Then they were on the deck of a small boat which tossed about in such a convincing gale that Buzz instinctively clutched his chair while Dikki, hand in his pockets, maintained a miraculous balance on the pitching deck. Then suddenly they were underwater, in oppressive silence, with a shark gliding between them and moss-covered ruins dim beyond the ribs of an ancient wreck.

Buzz found himself holding his breath before Dikki spoke and bursts of bubbles spewed from his mouth to jitter upward out of sight. "This is one of my favorites. It's so restful." A shimmering school of improbable tropicals darted and hovered about him for a moment, then shot away. "I could play with this thing all day," he said apologetically.

He fingered a stump of coral and was once again standing in a room: an open, low-ceilinged room with a balcony like the Roman villa, and graceful transparent furniture here and there. He seated himself in a low chair and leaned back: "Now, you have a show you wanted to tell me about."

"Is this one real?" Buzz asked.

"Almost. The furniture outline matches so we can use it, and the view from the balcony is real. The interior design is based on Korda's sets for *Things To Come.*"

"Is . . . all this what you've been doing for I.F.A.?"

"Well, most of what we just ran through I did on my own time. But they're paying lease and bank for the terminal, and I'm expected to familiarize myself with its capabilities as a creative tool. It's really a fantastic thing, Buzz."

"Yeah. I got that impression. I wouldn't mind having one to play with to compile a presentation for *Twenty Billion Monkeys on a Rock.*"

"That's your review? Tell me about it."

"Well, if I synthesized it, it'd be a rhythmic montage of bits. Maybe a dozen big numbers. Since the exsolars—you remember the exsolars—since they couldn't find any way to get to another planetary system, and their technology was far beyond ours, that means we aren't about to have any other planets to expand to either. And like monkeys who have bred to cover their isolated island, we have nothing left to do but talk to each other. I want to take a strand of continuous communication and string a series of numbers on it."

"I *like* that," said Dikki sincerely. "Got plots for specific sequences?"

"Some. I'd been thinking in terms of straight live-stage or holo presentation, but I could do a whole lot more with extensive synthing built into my ideation."

"You're fishing for an invitation to come down for a while. I'll bet Penta put you up to it. Sure—we've got lots of room now. It's really good to be able to move around and have some choice in the people you let near you. *You* should think about getting out of the city, Buzz. The population sinks are really going to hell. All the people who can't overcome the huddling instinct or sublimate it through their terminals will keep packing together until they succumb to Calhoun's Syndrome and fade out of the gene bank. Moral breakdown may be fun at the time, but it's not a healthy sign in a human society. Look, under Estate Rules we're allowed three short-time guests. How would you like to come down here for a week and work up that presentation? I won't need time on the Cineborg until I start a new project, and I can spare the storage while you're programming. I could even show it around for when you're ready. For 15 percent, of course."

"I'd want to haggle over that part, but if it includes the use of your Cineborg. . . . When can I come down?"

"Why not tonight, while it's fresh in your mind?"

Buzz thought of the message left with his phone and the call he had to make a little later. "Tonight's full," he said. "And Penta told me since Eden invited her she thought we might take the hydro down together. So I'll check with her tomorrow. Maybe by the end of the week. Why don't I give you a call when I know?" A formless reluctance had seized him, and he hesitated, inexplicably unwilling to commit himself.

"Okay. But make some notes on your million monkeys before those ideas get away. You should be doing a lot better than you are."

"Thanks. That's what Penta said. Maybe I will."

"That's it. Sayonara." A swirl of omnichromic fog blotted the scene, and Buzz was alone in his dim-lit cubicle. He opened the door and stepped out into the dusk.

There didn't seem to be anybody left in the park, and a chilly wind whipped up the slope around him. Suddenly Buzz felt lonely and oddly frightened. He hurried back across the grass to Pico and through the underpass to the light and warm shelter of Century Dome where familiar crowds moved and muttered. It wasn't until an hour later he remembered he hadn't looked up at the stars before coming inside.

The personal terminals and information network described in "Prognosis: Terminal" are not far-out at all; they could be built with today's technology. However, Dave wrote this in 1972, and at that time he was definitely making a prediction. It was a fairly safe one: That is, even in those days computer technology proceeded by leaps and bounds. What Dave didn't foresee was just how soon we could build all that. Neither did many others; things jumped a lot faster than most of us guessed.

In fact, by 2020 we could not only have the terminals

he describes, but have them implanted in our heads to speak directly into our auditory nerves.

Some of his other technology seems far-out, but I think of nothing he described that we could not have in the year 2020—provided, of course, that we do hold onto civilization that long.

A. E. Van Vogt is one of the giants of science fiction. He's also one of the few from the Golden Age of SF who are still regularly turning out stories. He's a big man, usually dressed in a superbly tailored suit. He lives in a big house full of splendid Oriental furniture. And he's one of the most fascinating people to talk with I've ever met.

I've been reading Van Vogt since high school, and because of him I spent the worst quarter of my academic life.

Eventually I got my revenge. Van had just published a book written solely to let him do an introductory blurb that proves, through a strange kind of formal logic, that "All men are Morton." By coincidence he was visiting my house just after I'd bought the book, and in a flash it came to me. I whipped out pen and paper and cast his sparkling statements into the most abstruse formal symbology I could manage. I drew heavily on Carnap's Sentential Calculus and used the most obscure notation I knew. Then wickedly I passed the paper over to Van, knowing full well that he couldn't read a line of it, as how many sane people can?

But it was genuine all right, and it was all Van's fault that I could do that to him. You see, about twenty years before, Van had written several classic stories

*about general semantics. I got hooked on them as many
of us did, and in due course I read Korzybski's* Science
and Sanity. *I wanted to know more about the subject;
and the fates arranged that there was at the University
of Iowa that quarter a noted expert on general semantics.
Naturally I rushed over to sign up for the only course
with him that I could manage. It was Formal Logic. For
graduate students.*

　　*"Future Perfect" is fairly typical Van Vogt: meaning
that about halfway through the story you won't be sure
you know what's going on. That's all right. Read on.
Pretty soon you'll really be confused. But it's all very
clear in the end. This is the story of the man who killed
the Golden Age . . . and why.*

future perfect

by a. e. van vogt

On that day that Steven Dalkins was eighteen years old,
he received an advisory letter from United Governments Life Credit that a million-dollar drawing account had been opened in his name. The congratulatory
cover note contained the usual admonitions for eigh-
teen-year-olds; gravely explained that the money being
made available to him—the million dollars—consti-
tuted his anticipated life earnings.

Spend it carefully; this may be all you will ever receive: That was the summation.

Dalkins was ready. In nine days, beginning on his
birthday, he spent $982,543.81. And he was wracking
his brain as to where he could dispose of the other
seventeen thousand when a treasury officer walked
into his lavish apartment and arrested him.

Dalkins put out his cigarette in a convenient ash-
tray—he was surprised to find one in the psychiatrist's
office—and then walked to the door the girl had indicated. He entered and paused with cynical respect,
waiting to be noticed.

The man behind the desk was about fifty, gaunt,
hair still without gray, and he was busy drawing lines
on a chart. Without looking up, he said, "Find yourself
a chair."

There were only two chairs to choose from. A hard-backed affair and a comfortable lounge type. With a sigh, Dalkins settled himself into the easy chair.

Without glancing up, Dr. Buhner said, "Wondered if you'd pick that one."

He made another line on the chart. Dalkins watched him despisingly. He was not alarmed. He had come to this interview expecting stereotyped responses. He was prepared for the verdict, whatever it might be. But the trivia was insulting.

He said with that sardonic respect, "You sent for me, Dr. Buhner."

That was an understatement. He had been delivered into this office by the law. His words received no answer. Dalkins shrugged, and leaned back prepared to wait.

The older man said, "Your reaction to that was quite interesting." He made a line on his chart.

Dalkins glared at the bent head. "Look here," he said angrily, "is this the way you treat human beings?"

"Oh, no." Promptly. "For legal purposes, we define a human being as an unalienated person. You are an alienated person. Therefore, legally you are not a human being."

Dalkins bristled, then caught himself. Cynically, he quoted, "Have I not hands, organs, dimensions, senses, affections, passions? fed with the same food . . . subject to the same diseases? . . ." He left the phrase unfinished, and waited for a reaction. He felt pleased with himself.

As before, Dr. Buhner spoke without looking up, "Strong word associations." The chart received its inevitable mark.

The older man straightened. For the first time, now, he raised his head. Bright, gray eyes gazed at Dalkins. "I have one question," he said. "Did you have a reason for spending that money within a ten-day period?"

The small, scrubbed-looking face of the boy sneered at him. "Wouldn't you like to know?" he asked sarcastically.

Dr. Buhner stood up. "Well, I think that does it. I shall recommend that you be fined whatever you purchased except two suits and accessories, and fined the seventeen thousand dollars of the balance remaining in your account. This will leave you a few hundred, and you may also keep your apartment. I should advise you that human beings may be sued for, or fined, as much as one hundred thousand dollars in any five-year period. Alienated persons of course lose everything when convicted. In your case, I plan to requisition one hundred dollars each week from the fine, to be paid to you if you show up at my office for therapy. No show, no one hundred dollars."

Dalkins laughed derisively. "You'll not ever see me again," he said, "unless you have me brought here by police action to listen to your phony analysis and stupid judgments."

The pyschiatrist stood gazing at him. If there was an expression on his hollow-cheeked face, it was not recognizable. Yet his next words seemed to indicate that Dalkins had penetrated his professional neutrality. He said, almost curtly, "All right, what *is* in your mind? What do you want?"

Dalkins was at the door, contemptuous. He stood there and he felt in himself a renewal of the greatness feeling that had made him act so decisively. For brief hours after his arrest the feeling had dimmed. There had even been a shadowy agreement in him with all the people who would regard as madness what he had done.

Never would he sink to such a doubt again.

The reaffirmation of his own rightness was in his voice now, as he said, "You had your chance. Next time tell Big Brother to use a man for a man's job. You muffed it, baby."

"Still," argued Dr. Buhner, who was very happy that this free-swinging dialogue had been triggered while the instruments were still focused and recording, "if I understood it, I could make things easier. I picture you as luxury-loving. No ascetic is Steven Dalkins."

Steven laughed. "I chose that easy chair because you expected me to. I got mad because you thought I would. I consciously fitted into your preconceptions. I don't fit them."

"Everybody fits in somewhere. Man's enduring structure permits only minor variations of personality and even of experience."

Steven shrugged.

Dr. Buhner hastily tried another tack. "What's wrong with every normal person receiving a million dollars on his eighteenth birthday? Everybody else thinks that and a number of similar developments are the millennium."

"Rumble on, little boy," said Steven Dalkins. "But when you're through, let me out of here. You're too late for this conversation. In future I talk only to the big boys."

Without waiting for a reply, Dalkins now opened the door. As he did so, the older man said, "As you leave, pause before the mirror in the anteroom and take a good look at who's talking about little boys."

"Okay, okay," said Dalkins. "So I'm only five feet six. So I don't even look eighteen."

"Maybe fifteen," interjected Buhner.

"In this instance," said Steven, "courage comes in a small package."

Pause, into which Steven projected: "And for your information, I am not an alienated person. And it's you that will have to make the decision to change, and not me."

Buhner smiled like a man who is accustomed to talking to people who think that it is thee not me who is irrational. He said, "If you're not alienated, I don't know who is."

He was talking to a closed door.

When the youth had gone, the psychiatrist sat down in his chair with that faint smile still on his face. He was joined by another man, who silently settled into the chair where Dalkins had sat a few minutes before.

"Well, you heard it all," said Buhner.

The other man pursed his rather full lips, and nodded.

"What do you make of it?"

The second man's answer was to stroke his jaw thoughtfully.

"He sounded sincere in the alienated fashion," said the psychiatrist.

Before his visitor could reply, or make a move, the door opened. The girl who had been in the anteroom came in with two copies of a computer printout. She handed one to each of the men, and went out.

There was a faint rustling of paper as Dr. Buhner and his guest scanned the information on the printout. The visitor folded his in a deliberate fashion, and for the first time spoke. "His physiologic reactions when you asked him that question," he said in a soft baritone, "establish that he did know about the ten-day lag between the time a lot of money is spent and a human being finds out about it."

"The information," was the reply, "is merely classified as special knowledge. It is not secret, but simply is not publicized. Tens of thousands of individuals learned of the delay in specific training they took."

The second man tapped the printout, which now lay on his lap. "I notice," he said, "he spent most of the money on the rapid production of a film. Any chance of it being worth anything?"

The gaunt man shook his head. "I had a committee of film people of diverse backgrounds look it over. Their report reinforced my own impression. It's a disjointed piece of junk. Apparently, none of the hastily assembled cast ever saw the whole script. They acted it out in bits and pieces. Clearly, the project was intended to spend the kind of large sum you can put into a film."

The visitor seemed nonplussed. "Have you ever had a case like this before?" he asked, bewildered.

"Once, with the difference that, when we traced down the expenditures, we discovered that he had tried to hide about fifty thousand and had paid another fifty out as a bribe."

"For heaven's sake"—in astonishment—"to whom?" When Dr. Buhner smilingly shook his head, the other man apologized. "Of course, the recipient was penalized and the incident is no longer on his record."

He broke off. "What's your next move with Dalkins?"

"We'll just have to wait and see. He has no hidden money. Therefore, the moment of truth should come rapidly."

"Still"—the visitor was thoughtful—"it says in the printout that his apartment is paid up for two months in advance. What's the state of the larder?"

"Lots of food."

"So he can live in total luxury for two months."

The specialist tapped the printout. "What bothers me," he said, "the computer agrees that he is not an alienated person."

Steven Dalkins came out of Dr. Buhner's office into a gleaming corridor, and along that corridor to an elevator, and so down to the ground floor. From there he sallied forth into a world that had not in fifty years changed much in appearance. There were the same buildings, or at least the same types of buildings. Glass, stone, brick, and plastic cast into various high-rise configurations. It differed from earlier eras in that it had told him every day in his conscious recollection that it was perfect.

The millennium had arrived. True, the eighteen-year-old recipient of a million dollars had to work until that sum was paid off. But, then, work was good for people; normal individuals didn't question that.

Most people never succeeded in paying off the debt; they simply didn't earn enough money. But they also, being unalienated, seldom spent all the money.

When an individual died, what was left of the million reverted to the state. The work debt, if any, was simultaneously wiped off the books. The children could only inherit a few personal effects, not money or property. There were no loose ends. Everybody started with a clean slate—and one million dollars. Legally, that sum could not be paid twice to anyone, nor could any portion thereof. The law did not provide alleviations for the condition in which Steven found himself. If he worked, his salary would automatically go to pay off his already existing debt.

Apparently unconcerned by any of this, Steven climbed into an electric taxi and was on his way.

In due course, the taxi turned onto the street beside the river and pulled into the driveway of a high-rise apartment building. Steven climbed out into the warm day, paid the driver, and then sauntered to the glittering front entrance. As he did so, he was aware of another car pulling to a stop across the road next to the river. The man in it got out and pretended to be interested in the river view.

The spy later reported to Dr. Buhner that "Mr. Dalkins entered the building in which is his apartment, and after two hours has not emerged."

The days went by, and he continued not to emerge.

After a week of nothing, the watchers out there shrugged, and said, in effect, "Well, why don't we just let things happen as they normally would for an eighteen?"

Accordingly, there arrived at Dalkins's apartment a notice from Computer-Mate. It informed him that a young woman, Stacy Aikens, age twenty-three, had been selected as a suitable marriage partner for him.

"As you probably know," the communication concluded, "after a computer selection, both parties have fourteen days to meet and either accept, or not accept, the selected person. If one selectee is willing and the other not, the willing individual is free and has three more opportunities to accept a marriage partner. On the other hand, the one who refused to accept the computer selectee has only two more chances.

"When the candidate has used up all three choices, one year must pass before another three opportunities are available. If in private life the candidate meets a potential life partner whose personal qualifications come within the frame of the computer programming for each of them, a marriage may also take place. It should be noticed that in this special situation Stacy Aikens has already waived the requirement that her alter-mate must have money.

"A potential candidate, who does not wish to be married at this time, should so advise Computer-Mate."

Dalkins did nothing. Neither objected, nor asked for his name to be withdrawn. He did not call the girl, and when she finally phoned him on the twelfth day he informed her that she was acceptable to him.

Apprised of these details. Dr. Buhner had another meeting with the representative of the Treasury Department. The man asked, "Do you think he'll marry the woman?"

Buhner smiled. "There we have him. To set his sex organs unlocked, he's got to. Evidently, whatever his plan, that much is important to him."

"Maybe all he wants is an opportunity to use up her cash."

The grim smile did not leave the psychiatrist's face. "No, we've already limited her withdrawals to exactly double what she has been living on up to now, with extra money available on special request for specific purposes. No, no"—he shook his head—"when biology solved the problem of locking up the male sex organ, and later opening it up so that it could function only with one woman—his wife—the entire course of family relations and in fact human history was altered in a positive fashion. And of course since women live an average of seven years longer than men, we naturally set it up so that our youths must marry girls who are four to seven years older than they are."

He concluded, "My bet is, he shows up for the wedding ceremony."

The sign above the doors read: HORMONIC COMPENSATION CENTER and ALTERNATE MARRIAGE REGISTRATION. There was a lineup in front of the doors when Dalkins arrived. A group of males stood on one side of a long narrow fencelike barrier, and a group of women on the other. With one exception, the males were all boys in their late teens and the females all young women in their early twenties. The exception among the men was an individual of about forty. When Dalkins arrived, no women of corresponding age had shown up among the females; so he assumed that the man was there to spy on him. Dalkins smiled contemptuously.

He took his place at the rear of the male lineup and glanced over at the women on the other side of the fence. At once he saw Stacy Aikens. The young woman had already seen him and was gazing eagerly in his direction. Their gazes met. It was the first time they had seen each other in the flesh; and it occurred to Dalkins that he had better smile. He smiled. She smiled back, revealing rather large teeth.

Stacy left her place in the lineup—she was in third position from the door—and, as required by the rules, came back opposite him in tenth position. The way she walked back toward him indicated that she had very short legs.

Dalkins was not critical of her physical appearance. The new-style thinking about such things had been around for more than forty years; and in spite of his antagonism to part of the world around him, that one he had not noticed. The new-style thinking required that all normal girls, women, boys, and men be considered beautiful without exception.

So appearance, in terms of what old-style thinking would have called beauty, was not a factor in computer mating. Height was. Weight was. Age was. And so the young woman who now stood just across the barrier from Steven was 5 feet, 1 inch tall (to his 5 feet, 6 inches), 100½ pounds to his 128, and 5 years older than he.

All over the world fatties married fatties, thinnies

thinnies, and intermediates other middlings. And of course the ridiculous tendency that men had once had to marry females younger than themselves was nullified by an exact-opposite system based on good sense and the findings of biochemistry. Sexually, as economically, it was the millennium.

Soon they were inside the building and were seated in adjoining booths, visible to each other and to the boys and young women in other booths through thick, transparent plastic. Since, at Steven's insistence, they had opted for the alternate marriage, they signed a plastic plate with a special type of pen. Their signature was automatically transferred by the computer to the distant department of vital statistics in the state capitol. The signature, of itself, was the marriage ceremony, requiring only the medical recompensation of the male and second step of harmonic alignment to make it legal and permanent.

At the computer's request, Dalkins unzipped the right hip of his special marriage trousers. Then he leaned back, also by request, and waited while he was strapped in by two mechanical hands. As the hands withdrew, a glasslike structure fronted by a needle and a beam of light focused on his exposed thigh just below the hip. The needle moved slowly and entered the flesh. The red fluid visible in the transparent needle disappeared inside him. The needle withdrew.

The computer said, "Hold your arm steady for Step Two."

Dalkins, who had located the older man, saw that he was standing a few feet away watching the "marriage ceremony," and saw that in fact the man seemed so convinced that all was going well that he had half-turned away.

Now! thought Dalkins.

The pix-phone rang. Dr. Buhner pressed the button that connected the tiny receiver in his ear and said, "Dr. Buhner here."

The picture that formed on the pix-plate was that of his erstwhile visitor and confidante. The man said in a fretful voice, "Roosley at this end. What went wrong?"

Buhner could not fail to notice the accusing tone of blame, and he said, "We must first of all have an understanding, you and I."

"About what?" Astonished voice and face.

"I had no control over that situation. The law does not permit it."

"You had your observer on the scene."

Buhner ignored the second assignment of blame. "Have I made my position clear?"

"Yes, yes." Resignedly.

"What happened," said Dr. Buhner in a brisker tone, "is that again our Steven seems to have taken the trouble to discover in advance the details of a process that most people go through without preknowledge."

"When it was done to me," said Roosley, "I was in a locked room, strapped into a chair. I didn't have a chance to get away."

"If," said Dr. Buhner, "you had brought along a computer repairman's key and an automatic pistol to shoot your way through a locked door—"

There was an impressed expression on the face in the pix screen. Finally: "What are you going to do?"

"Nothing."

"Why not?" Sharply.

"There's no law against what Steven did."

"You mean, you can deactivate a machine, and shoot your way out of a locked building?"

"Hormonic Compensation may sue him for damages,

but since he has no money it will do them no good."

"B-but," his caller protested, "isn't it illegal to be in the condition Steven is in now, a sexually free male?"

"No."

"But—" the other man groped.

"It is required by law that a male child reaching the age of puberty have his sex-performance capacity placed under control. It is required by law that he can get married, since marriage is a man-made relationship, only if he goes through the process of being recompensated and aligned with his future wife. If this does not happen, then no marriage has legally taken place. You see," Dr. Buhner continued, "the technique for all this has been taken from the old Chinese Communist People's Army concept, except of course there's no death penalty. But it's simply now, as then, a trap for the unwary individual who, in both the Communist and in our situation, was a teenage male still in a naïve stage. Before he can think, we capture him sexually. Before he can grow up, we align him sexually with his future wife, and the law states that once this is done it cannot be undone. The state is justified in taking these arbitrary steps because its goal is a peaceful, hard-working populace."

Pause.

"Where's Steven's wife now?"

"She's not married. The final step was not completed. She has returned to her own apartment."

"And where is Steven?"

"He has not yet returned to his apartment."

Roosley said after a pause, "As I understand it, for the first time in a quarter of a century a male is out there"—he made a vague gesture with his arm, taking in half the horizon—"who is able to perform the sex act with more than one woman?"

"That used to be the way every male was."

"And that is not illegal?"

"No, it is merely undesirable. But it's a natural state. No natural human state has ever been specifically declared to be illegal."

The face on the pix-screen, in the course of a few moments of contemplating the potentialities of the situation, had acquired a distinct mottled look. The man muttered, "But good God, one man and *all* those unmarried girls and women between eighteen and twenty-three!"

"It could be," soothed Dr. Buhner, "that seduction is not his purpose. For that he didn't have to get rid of his money."

Roosley said blankly, "But what could be his purpose?"

"My assistants," said the psychiatrist, "are continuing to check into Steven's background, trying to find a clue."

"What do you think he will do now?"

"He seems to have covered his tracks well," the older man admitted reluctantly. "I have no report on him. Maybe he's woman-chasing."

Roosley made a choking sound in his throat. And broke the connection.

Buhner hesitated, then dialed a very special number. This time, when there was a click, no face came on the pix screen, but a man's voice—deep, determined, interested—said, "I've read your report, Doctor. I agree that Steven should receive publicity. If your prediction about him does not come true, at least we'll have made our first try this decade. Good luck."

Steven sat on his buttocks on the grass, his back against a tree at the edge of the park, and stared up into the sky. It was a pose. Actually, he was keeping a sharp lookout for possible spies. He was not entirely certain that he had got away without being seen. He presumed that the treasury lords would like to find out how he proposed to survive without money.

"It's easy," he called out to altogether four suspicious-looking men who walked by while he sat there (as if they would understand his meaning). "The world pays more for creativity and most for rebellion. Tell that to your masters."

One of the four, a puzzled individual of about thirty, came over, and said, "Hey, you're the fellow who gave away your million, according to the news report. Why?"

Steven said, dazzled and delighted, "You mean they're giving me publicity?" He caught himself, shrugged, said, "Move along, bub. If you don't know why, telling you wouldn't do any good."

About dusk, Steven came lazily to his feet. Sauntering—in case there was a watcher—he walked back into the park to where a tiny stream flowed into a culvert. Bending, he reached into the darkness of the culvert, groped, and then straightened. In one hand he now held a waterproof container. From its interior he drew a rolled-up sign. This, like a sandwich man of old, he slipped over his head. The front of the sign was a white canvas with a message on it. The message was:

> I'm Steve Dalkins, the nut
> who gave away his million
> dollars.

The back of the sign, also canvas, read:

> I invite you to hear my
> story any night at West
> Park, eight o'clock.

That part didn't mean what it said. Maybe, if it could be arranged, he'd send somebody over there in case people showed. But the purpose would be to mislead possible observers.

Steven walked along, confident, smiling. The sky grew dark, and the sidewalks began to give off the light they had accumulated during the day. Walls of stores glowed in the same way. People walked up, glanced at him and his sign, and moved past. Most gave some kind of disapproving indication; but the alert Dalkins noticed one here, one there, who had a different reaction.

To each of these, if it could be done, he spoke quietly in a low voice, "We've got to do something—right? Meet me any night at the. . . ." And he named another park. The biggest moment of the evening occurred when a young man with a flushed face briefly fell in step beside him, and said, "You got a plan for beating these bastards?"

"Sure have," said Steven.

The young man did something twisty with his body. It was a gesture that had in it an infinite hostility. "I'm with you, and I'll bring my gang. My name is Jack."

"Good."

The group that first night at ten consisted of eight single responders, including two young women, and a surprisingly large group of seven intense young men and four equally sincere young women. This was Jack's "gang."

There were no questions of why. Each male and female *knew* that this had to be done. Each was relieved that someone had at last taken the step of no return.

It was as if they all understood the reality of things deep inside their viscera, and *that* part was taken for granted. Only the details of what to do needed to be worked out. And, of course, there Steven had his plan.

They organized Overthrow Associates that first night. It was agreed that Steven Dalkins would be recompensed for his lost million. Each person present at the founders meeting wrote him a check for one thousand dollars. All future members—it was authorized—would be assessed the same amount entirely on behalf of Steven.

"You may not get back your full million," said the flush-faced man, Jack Brooks, "but surely we can get together as many determined persons as were behind the assassins of Alexander the Second of Russia in the 1880s. Surely, five hundred is not too much to expect."

"I think there'll be more than that," said Steven noncommittally.

At the end of Month One, there were 2,782 members. Each member during Month Two was given the task of locating five more alienated persons. Since the receipts totaled more than a million, Steve said he would donate the difference to expenses. He had confided the first step of his plan to a small inner circle of the conspiracy, which included Jack. These individuals told inquiring members that the plan was "the greatest," but that it would be unwise to reveal its details to any but key figures.

Overthrow Associates had 53,064 members when, shortly after the end of Month Four, it undertook its first act of total defiance.

The authorities had decided to publicize Steven's condition. Girls and women were urged, if they were approached by a small young man to call the police if he manifested ulterior motives. Buhner, in his reports, doubted if any woman would be resistant to the charms of a sexually free male. However—he suggested—Steven couldn't be sure of that, and so he would be the careful one.

Nevertheless, the psychiatrist, when he lay awake at night, felt somewhat more restless than was usual for him.

Daytimes he monitored Steven's progress by the number of checks that were made out to him. As the total grew, a shiver of anxiety almost visibly oscillated through those members of the United Governments who, by agreement, had to be kept informed of such matters.

Whenever people got too nervous they contacted Buhner. This particular morning the caller had a beefy face with an edgy voice that said, "What are you doing about these rascals?"

"We're getting ready for a cleanup."

"How do you mean?"

Buhner explained. Police were turning their attention from routine, and pointing toward an elemental force. Out of the woodwork of the society, a strange breed of human creatures were emerging. The tense, determined individuals were drawn into the light by a common impulse to smash an environment that, in some obscure way, had angered them.

Their nonconformist impulse to do violence had its own purity. They loved each other and were loyal to their group leaders. In earlier decades, there had been other dramatic actions to motivate affection for and obedience to one or more leaders. In this instance, *this* year, they were proud to be associated with someone who had had the will to give away his million dollars. After that, nobody vaguely questioned the right of Ste ven Dalkins to be "the boss."

That made it easy for the police. All the checks were made out to one man. The signatures were written plain to see. Every man, boy, girl, and woman was identified; and the computers sent printouts to police centers across the land. Quietly, detectives visited each person's neighborhood, and located him or her, exactly.

The society, of course, did not permit people to be arrested merely because they wrote a check to Steven Dalkins. There had to be an association with an illegal action.

"But what can they do to a perfect world?" That was the question most often asked of Dr. Buhner, and here it was again. He made the same statement now as he had in the past. "Twelve years ago Charley Huyck led a revolt aimed at our computer-education system. Twenty-three years ago the rebellion of the Gilbert brothers had as its target the group method of electing politicians. After each outbreak, *all* of the participants were arrested, charged with being alienated persons, convicted, and disposed of."

"What," asked the heavy-faced VIP, "do you think Dalkins will attack?"

"Something more basic is my feeling."

"For God's sake," exploded the politician, "what could be more basic than an attack on the political system?"

"Well," temporized Buhner diplomatically.

The edgy voice calmed, and said, "Do you think Dalkins is aware that you can follow up all those checks?"

"Yes, I think he knows, because he has transferred some of the money over to a company."

"Oh, that! But, surely, in this special situation—"

Buhner shook his head firmly. "How companies spend their money cannot be checked on, because it might give a tip to their competition. The computer system would either have to be reprogrammed or a public statement would have to be made by the authorities. But we don't want to do that. We want to catch all of these people and get rid of them."

That night, as Buhner lay awake, he was disturbed to realize that slightly over four months had gone by. So if Roosley's fantasies had been even approximately true, then it was time for violated virgins to be showing up in small hordes. What was disturbing was the possibility that there weren't any . . . could it be, he asked himself, that Steven has been behaving like a responsible person all these months and has *not* been out there on a seduction spree?

But if not that, what had he been doing?

The next morning looked absolutely delightful when he glanced out of the window of his high-rise apartment. The sky was as blue as a brightly lighted tidal pool . . . a little later, he was peacefully, and unsuspectingly, eating a delicious meat-substitute breakfast when the red emergency light flashed on his media set. The alarm buzzer sounded. Then a young man walked onto the stage at which the camera pointed. He said: "Ladies and gentlemen, do not be alarmed. This is a message from Overthrow Associates. We have temporarily taken over the principal broadcast centers of the American continent. We want to tell you something our leader, Steven Dalkins, believes you would like to know."

He thereupon explained and demonstrated (on himself and a girl who suddenly appeared) the chemical method whereby the sex alignment of a man and wife could be terminated. He named several locations where the chemical could be secured locally, and said that similar messages were being broadcast from the other stations across the land.

He urged: "Have your check for one thousand dollars ready, and remember this may be your only chance to get the little case of syringes with the compensating shots in them. You can buy them now and decide later if you'll actually use them. If you're a person of decision you'll act at once before there is any interference with the sale, and think later."

One of these locations named was about a mile from Buhner's apartment. In seconds he was out of the door and heading groundward in a high-speed elevator.... outside, he ran for an electric taxi. En route, he wrote out his check. Even as it was, by the time he had paid the taxi fare several hundred men and about fifty women were crowding around a helicopter which stood at the edge of a small park. As Buhner pushed forward, waving his check as the others were doing with theirs, he saw that three girls and four men were passing out small boxes and another man and girl were taking the checks, examining them, putting them into a metal container.

The psychiatrist was barely in time. He handed over his check, waited nervously while it was scrutinized, and then grabbed the box that was held out to him. He was still backing away, clutching the precious kit protectively, when one of the young people yelled a warning: "The police are coming. Beat it, everybody!"

In bare seconds, the nine were inside with their cartons and their checks. As the door started to close, the machine lifted into the sky like a scared falcon. Up there it looked exactly like the dozens of other craft like it in which buyers had arrived and which had for many minutes been taking off from all the surrounding streets.

Buhner arrived at his office looking disheveled, but he made his report to Top Level feeling triumphant. The report from the government laboratory later that day confirmed that the seven syringes of the kit he had bought did indeed contain the dealignment chemical.

According to a still later report from the computer network, Overthrow Associates sold 883,912 kits that day at 6,224 locations for one thousand dollars each. And the checks were all made out to Steven Dalkins.

Power and money cast long shadows. The images in the minds of certain shocked persons flickered with the possibility that the next allotment of chemicals would bring in eight billion, or even *eighty*.

It was too much. The rumors came to Steven's ears. He thought: *the turning point!* That very day he dialed the computer code that connected him to his followers everywhere in a closed circuit. He placed himself in front of the pix camera.

There he stood. His eyes were small gray marbles bright with intelligence. His checks were flushed. His small body was tense. He glared into the eyepiece striving to fix every viewer out there with his determined gaze.

He explained the views of the shocked members, whose leader was Jack Brooks, and he finished, "Jack's vision has proved greater than mine. Every man has his limitations. What has already happened seems to be just about what I'm capable of. So—"

He paused dramatically, then made his firm statement.

"I hereby resign any control that I have had of Overthrow Associates in favor of my dear friend, Jack Brooks. I give you all my love and best wishes."

He finished graciously, "I'll still sign checks for all valid purchases for the next move of the organization. For that you can always reach me on the code. Good-bye to all you wonderful people."

As Steven's voice and face faded, in a distant apartment a young man with a red face that was positively
scarlet grabbed his own pix-phone, dialed a number,
and yelled into it, "Steven, you so-and-so, what do you
mean—valid purchases? I want a total power-of-attor-
ney over the cash in your account, except for maybe
ten million. Show your sincerity."

They were on a private line, so Steven said, "If I
don't retain control of the money, you might be tempted
to do something against me."

"Sign over twenty-eight million right now to pay for
the next allotment," screamed Jack.

"Okay," said Steven.

When it was done, Jack Brooks paced the floor. "That
s.o.b.," he said, "is going to get away with over eight
hundred million dollars."

He stopped pacing, scowled, said, "Like hell he is."
He walked to the pix-phone again. This time he called
Dr. Buhner, and said, "Every evening at dusk Steven
Dalkins takes a walk in one of the parks."

The psychiatrist had at least three meetings to at-
tend, while he considered what he would do with the
tipoff. . . .

First, with computer engineers and adminstrative
staff. The question: Were the great thinking machines
programmed to check out 883,000 names?

The answer: There were endless flows of exact logic,
total information somewhere, every transaction of
every person available, not a single natural barrier in
the entire system—so, yes.

Buhner's second meeting was with the directors of
the biochemist guild. They had an analysis for him on
the basis of one clue. A long-time employee, who was

not a member of the trust group that controlled the sexual dealignment ingredient (one of seven) manufactured at the plant where he worked, had quit his job a few months ago. Investigation had shown that he had made a secret, unofficial study of chemistry over many years.

"We may speculate," concluded the board, "that a group of seven or more persons either separately motivated or in a conspiracy sought employment in such laboratories long ago, and bided their information until someone like Dalkins came along."

Buhner's third meeting was with a committee of the United Governments. A leading economist explained in a shaky voice to the distracted members of the committee that the million-dollars-to-everybody system depended on the statistical reality that the needs of the populace be consistent. An additional expenditure of one thousand dollars per person by a sizable percentage of adults must not happen.

No question, thought Buhner, Steven has hit the perfect world a blow below the belt—

The problem was, what to do about it? In his own speech, he said cautiously, "It would appear as if the attempt to control mankind's genitalia has been nullified by Steven Dalkins as an incidental act in the accomplishment of a secret goal of his own."

He pointed out—when eight hundred thousand persons did a similar act of vandalism against a system, then by theory the system must be examined and not the individual.

He made his recommendations and concluded, "I refrain from offering a solution for Steven himself. Vague rumor has it that he is trying to break off his connection with his followers. That may not be easy to do."

At noon the next day, the United Governments is-
sued a determined voiced statement through their
elected secretary:

It has been deemed inadvisable to permit 883,000
males to prey on a hundred million unmarried
young women. The United Governments accordingly authorize drug outlets to make available
hormonic decompensation kits to those persons
over eighteen who choose to unalign themselves
with their spouses. The price of the kit shall be
ten dollars. The names of all persons who make
this choice will be publicly available. If individuals who have already purchased the kits turn
them in before the end of the current month, their
names will not be among the posted.

As Jack Brooks heard those fateful words, he leaped
to his feet and charged against the nearest wall of his
apartment, hitting it with one shoulder. Flung off by
the force of his violent action, he threw himself at another wall. Presently exhausted, he sank into a chair
and brooded on the reality that no one who could pay
ten dollars would buy the same product for one thousand dollars.

His fantasy of eight billion was now a mere foam of
rage in his clenched mouth. The rage was directed entirely at one person: Steven. Steven must have known
this would happen . . . how can we get even with that—
that—that?

Steven Dalkins, all fourteen of him, took his usual
evening workout shortly after dusk. At least, those
were the reports relayed back to Buhner by the agents
he sent to each of the city parks.

Could one of the fourteen be Steven himself? It didn't really matter for Buhner's purposes. He stood across the street from the public pathway of one of the parks, and watched a five-foot-six-inch youth jog toward him. If it was Steven, he was well disguised. A good makeup job concealed every significant feature of his face.

As this particular Steven came opposite him, the psychiatrist walked rapidly across the street. "Please tell Mr. Dalkins," he said loudly, "that Dr. Buhner would like him to call. Tell him he's now going to have to admit why he did all this—"

That was as far as he got. Dalkins turned in midstride, ran across the street, and then along the sidewalk. Suddenly, he seemed to see what he wanted. He darted to a car by the curb just as a woman was climbing into it. There seemed to be some struggle between them, which Dalkins won. The car started up. The last thing Buhner saw was the machine receding down the street, with Dalkins at the wheel and the woman lying back against the seat. Her head rolled limply and she slipped out of sight.

Buhner's men found the abandoned car twenty minutes later with the dead body of the woman lying on the floor of the front seat.

"Let him get out of *that!*" said Jack Brooks when the news was phoned to him by the murderer. His flushed face smirked into a grimacing smile. "Sending out fourteen Stevens was the smartest idea I've had up to now."

He was feeling better for another reason. There was a possibility that a percentage of men would be willing to sign over a car or other property in exchange for the kit rather than pay ten dollars and be identifiable and on a list. It was too bad that there was no cash in the perfect world and that every money transaction had to be by computer credit, but still—he shrugged—there was always a way.

The murder was announced over the news media; the circumstances described.

It was a quarter of four when Steven phoned Dr. Buhner.

Later—

Carrying his equipment, the psychiatrist arrived at the prearranged rendezvous. A man at the door guided him to a large, tastefully decorated anteroom. The pretty girl there escorted him through a door to a large inner office and closed the door behind her as she departed.

Silently, Buhner set up his equipment, then faced the youth who sat behind a gleaming desk. Steven Dalkins waved him at the two vacant chairs, one soft and one hard. The M.D. settled into the hard chair.

"Hmm," said Steven, "I was wondering which one you would choose."

He leaned back with a twisted smile on his small face. "How does it feel, Doc, to have someone giving you that superior treatment?"

Dr. Buhner stared at him with his pale gray eyes, and said, "Steven, slightly over forty thousand members of Overthrow Associates had been arrested by the time I started out for your place."

"This is only one of my places," said Steven.

The older man ignored the interruption. "Four out of five have already elected to go voluntarily to one of the space colonies. That way they can keep their money for sure." He smiled grimly. "Not everyone cares to gamble his million."

"So only I am in jeopardy?"

"Steven," said Buhner tensely, "who could have killed, or ordered the killing, of that woman?" As the silence lengthened, Buhner said, "Maybe we've already got him in custody and can verify your story in a few seconds." He indicated the machines that were focused on the genius boy in front of him, and urged, "Steven, you mustn't be loyal to someone who's trying to pin a murder on you."

"What happens to a convicted murderer?" asked Steven, after another pause.

"Nobody is convicted of murder in our day," was the reply. "The *only* crime is alienation."

"All right, what happens to a person convicted of alienation?"

"That's classified information."

"The rumor is that they're executed. Is that true?"

"I'm not a member of the board that handles that. I've heard the rumor." Buhner smiled his grim smile. "Now that you've met some of them, Steven, what would you do with alienated individuals?"

Steven hesitated. "It's unfair," he said finally, "for the unalienated to pass judgment on those persons who through some accident of childhood trauma got to be alienated."

"But you noticed?"

There was a faraway expression in the boy's eyes. "Many of them are exceptionally warmhearted," he temporized.

Buhner refused to be sidetracked. "Steven, how many murders that you heard about were committed by your followers in the past four months?"

The barest shadow of a sad smile was suddenly on Steven's face. "Most of them are alienated about other things," he said, "but those who are alienated that way killed about eight hundred persons."

"Why? Did you find out why they did it?"

"The victims said or did something that violated the ideals of the murderer."

"And so," said Buhner with the touch of grief in his voice that he always felt at such revelations, "in this great universe where a man's life so far as we know is only a tiny span of years, they in their inner fury of rightness denied even that short a time to nearly a thousand human beings. Tell me, what should be done with people like that?"

Once more, their gazes met. This time, the boy looked away quickly. And there seemed no question. The four months of close contact with the endless twists and distortions of truths of the alienated persons he had known had left their scarring marks.

On his face was the consequent judgment.

Steven said, "His name is Jack Brooks."

Buhner pressed some buttons on his machinery, watched the dials briefly, then said: "He's among the captured." Once more, manipulation, followed by the comment: "The computer is asking him if he ordered, or committed, the murder. He denies it. But his heart, his lungs, his liver, his blood vessels, tell a different story."

Their gazes met across the control instrument. "Well, Steven," said the older man, "I've been proceeding on the assumption that you're an unalienated person, and that therefore—though it would be a little hard to imagine what it could be—you have some deep-meaning reason for what you have done."

Steven said, "I should like you to accompany me somewhere."

"Could you use some reliable witnesses?"

"Yes."

Buhner and the United Governments' secretary, and

Roosley, and two other important persons stood behind a tree on one side of a tree-lined street as Steven walked across to a small suburban house on the other.

He stopped outside the gate and whistled twice long and twice short.

A minute went by. Then the door of the house opened.

Out of it there emerged a rapidly moving figure of a young girl. A child? No. She charged over to Steven Dalkins and flung her small body against his small body with an impact that sent him back several steps. The two—the dynamic girl and the high-energy boy—thereupon proceeded to hit one mouth against the other, and to squeeze their bodies together in a series of minor but definite blows.

"Good God!" said Buhner involuntarily. "He did all this in order to marry a girl his own age."

As if he had heard the words, or deduced that they would be spoken or thought, Steven turned and called out into the gathering dusk, "But it's not illegal; not now."

"Love," mumbled the psychiatrist. "I haven't thought of anything like that since I gave up little Esther when *I* was eighteen."

Suddenly, his legs wouldn't hold him. He lay down there on the grass, vaguely aware of the others bending over him anxiously.

It was ridiculous, of course, but the shameful tears streamed down his cheeks. . . . After all, he chided himself, little Esther would now be big Esther, married and with a brood of Estherettes. And, besides, it was well known that people always outgrew age-eighteen attachments.

The arguments, so cogently true, flapped unheeded through his head. The feeling that had leaped at him out of his forgotten past somehow conveyed the wordless meaning that he had never been given the chance to grow through those emotions. Muttering, Buhner struggled to his feet, shook away helping hands, and hurried off along the darkening street.

He had important things to do, like recovering from thirty years of living without love.

The Science Fiction Encyclopedia *says "Norman Spinrad has been a refreshing, iconoclastic force in modern SF, and a convincing analyst of some of the more apocalyptic tendencies in modern American life." It also rates "A Thing of Beauty" as "possibly Spinrad's best story altogether."*

I thoroughly agree. When I became president of Science Fiction Writers of America (a weird situation; they needed an experienced administrator, and I was elected president the year I joined SFWA), Norman was my vice-president. He lived about a mile from me, and we often met to discuss SFWA affairs. He had a strange quirk: He'd come up with ideas that didn't quite fit the situation, and if you tried to argue with him, he'd defend passionately. I soon learned the remedy: Don't argue. Just listen. Within half an hour he'd talk himself out of the unsuitable and transform the whole concept into something extremely valuable. I also learned that he knows everybody.

Norman has had a checkered career. He was once one of the fee readers for a literary agency; his instructions were never to discourage anyone. Tell them the story was "almost good enough to publish," and get them to send it back rewritten with more money. Of course Norman couldn't stand that and was fired when the owner's

227

brother found Norman had written a letter to a hopeless case advising a ten-year vacation from writing.

He was also known as a New Wave writer, but his stories have such Old Wave characteristics as a beginning, middle, and end, and a plot; if the New Wave movement had consisted of Spinrads it probably wouldn't have been so controversial. He also caused the leading British New Wave magazine, New Worlds, *to be banned from the major English bookstores; they thought his fine novel* Bug Jack Baron *too obscene, although, measured by today's standards, it's rather tame. The novel almost won a Hugo, and probably would have had it not been up against Ursula LeGuin's* Left Hand of Darkness.

This story was written for this collection. When you've finished it you won't know whether to laugh or cry; at least I don't. But I'm pleased to have Bugged Norman Spinrad into writing what many consider his finest story.

a thing of beauty

by norman spinrad

"There's a gentleman by the name of Mr. Shiburo Ito to see you," my intercom said. "He is interested in the purchase of an historic artifact of some significance."

While I waited for him to enter my private office, I had computcentral display his specs on the screen discreetly built into the back of my desk. My Mr. Ito was none other than Ito of Ito Freight Boosters of Osaka; there was no need to purchase a readout from Dun & Bradstreet's private banks. If Shiburo Ito of Ito Boosters wrote a check for anything short of the national debt, it could be relied upon not to bounce.

The slight, balding man who glided into my office wore a black-silk kimono with a richly brocaded black obi, Mendocino needlepoint by the look of it. No doubt, back in the miasmic smog of Osaka, he bonged the peons with the latest skins from Saville Row. Everything about him was *just so;* he purchased confidently on that razor edge between class and ostentation that only the Japanese can handle with such grace, and then only when they have millions of hard yen to back them up. Mr. Ito would be no sucker. He would want whatever he wanted for precise reasons all his own and would not be budgeable from the center of his desires. The typical heavyweight Japanese businessman, a prime example of the breed that's pushed us out of the center of the international arena.

Mr. Ito bowed almost imperceptibly as he handed me his card. I countered by merely bobbing my head in his direction and remaining seated. These face and posture games may seem ridiculous, but you can't do business with the Japanese without playing them.

As he took a seat before me, Ito drew a black cylinder from the sleeve of his kimono and ceremoniously placed it on the desk before me.

"I have been given to understand that you are a connoisseur of Fillmore posters of the early to mid-1960s period, Mr. Harris," he said. "The repute of your collection has penetrated even to the environs of Osaka and Kyoto, where I make my habitation. Please permit me to make this minor addition. The thought that a contribution of mine may repose in such illustrious surroundings will afford me much pleasure and place me forever in your debt."

My hands trembled as I unwrapped the poster. With his financial resources, Ito's polite little gift could be almost anything but disappointing. My daddy loved to brag about the old expense-account days when American businessmen ran things, but you had to admit that the fringe benefits of business Japanese-style had plenty to recommend them.

But when I got the gift open, it took a real effort not to lose points by whistling out loud. For what I was holding was nothing less than a mint example of the very first Grateful Dead poster in subtle black and gray, a super-rare item, not available for any amount of sheer purchasing power. I dared not inquire as to how Mr. Ito had acquired it. We simply shared a long, silent moment contemplating the poster, its beauty and historicity transcending whatever questionable events might have transpired to bring us together in its presence.

How could I not like Mr. Ito now? Who can say that the Japanese occupy their present international position by economic might alone?

"I hope I may be afforded the opportunity to please your sensibilities as you have pleased mine, Mr. Ito," I finally said. That was the way to phrase it; you didn't thank them for a gift like this, and you brought them around to business as obliquely as possible.

Ito suddenly became obviously embarrassed, even furtive. "Forgive me my boldness, Mr. Harris, but I have hopes that you may be able to assist me in resolving a domestic matter of some delicacy."

"A domestic matter?"

"Just so. I realize that this is an embarrassing intrusion, but you are obviously a man of refinement and infinite discretion, so if you will forgive my forwardness..."

His composure seemed to totally evaporate, as if he was going to ask me to pimp for some disgusting perversion he had. I had the feeling that the power had suddenly taken a quantum jump in my direction, that a large financial opportunity was about to present itself.

"Please feel free, Mr. Ito...."

Ito smiled nervously. "My wife comes from a family of extreme artistic attainment," he said. "In fact, both her parents have attained the exalted status of National Cultural Treasures, a distinction of which they never tire of reminding me. While I have achieved a large measure of financial success in the freight-booster enterprise, they regard me as *nikulturi*, a mere merchant, severely lacking in esthetic refinement as compared to their own illustrious selves. You understand the situation, Mr. Harris?"

I nodded as sympathetically as I could. These Japs certainly have a genius for making life difficult for themselves! Here was a major Japanese industrialist shrinking into low posture at the very thought of his sponging in-laws, whom he could probably buy and sell out of petty cash. At the same time, he was obviously out to cream the sons-of-bitches in some crazy way that would only make sense to a Japanese. Seems to me the Japanese are better at running the world than they are at running their lives.

"Mr. Harris, I wish to acquire a major American artifact for the gardens of my Kyoto estate. Frankly, it must be of sufficient magnitude so as to remind the parents of my wife of my success in the material realm every time they should chance to gaze upon it and I shall display it in a manner which will assure that they gaze upon it often. But of course it must be of sufficient beauty and historicity so as to prove to them that my taste is no less elevated than their own. Thus shall I gain respect in their eyes and reestablish tranquillity in my household. I have been given to understand that you are a valued counselor in such matters, and I am eager to inspect whatever such objects you may deem appropriate."

So that was it! He wanted to buy something big enough to bong the minds of his artsy-fartsy relatives, but he really didn't trust his own taste—he wanted me to show him something he would want to see. And he was swimming like a goldfish in a sea of yen! I could hardly believe my good luck. How much could I take him for?

"Ah . . . what size artifact did you have in mind, Mr. Ito?" I asked as casually as I could.

"I wish to acquire a major piece of American monumental architecture so that I may convert the gardens of my estate into a shrine to its beauty and historicity. Therefore a piece of classical proportions is required. Of course it must be worthy of enshrinement, otherwise an embarrassing loss of esteem will surely ensue."

"Of course."

This was not going to just another Howard Johnson or gas-station sale; even something like an old Hilton or the Cooperstown Baseball Hall of Fame I unloaded last year was thinking too small. In his own way, Ito was telling me that price was no object; the sky was the limit. This was the dream of a lifetime! A sucker with a bottomless bank account placing himself trustingly in my tender hands!

"Should it please you, Mr. Ito," I said, "we can inspect several possibilities here in New York immediately. My jumper is on the roof."

"Most gracious of you to interrupt your most busy schedule on my behalf, Mr. Harris. I would be delighted."

I lifted the jumper off the roof, floated her to a thousand feet, then took a mach 1.5 jump south over the decayed concrete jungles at the tip of Manhattan. The curve brought us back to float about a mile north of Bedloe's Island. I took her down to three hundred and brought her in toward the Statue of Liberty at a slow drift, losing altitude imperceptibly as we crept up on the Headless Lady, so that by the time we were just offshore, we were right down on the deck. It was a nice touch to make the goods look more impressive—manipulating the perspectives so that the huge, green, headless statue, with its patina of firebomb soot, seemed to rise up out of the bay like a ruined colossus as we floated toward it.

Mr. Ito betrayed no sign of emotion. He stared straight ahead out the bubble without so much as a word or a flicker or gesture.

"As you are no doubt aware, this is the famous Statue of Liberty," I said. "Like most such artifacts, it is available to any buyer who will display it with proper dignity. Of course I would have no trouble convincing the Bureau of National Antiquities that your intentions are exemplary in this regard."

I set the autopilot to circle the island at fifty yards offshore so that Ito could get a fully rounded view, and see how well the statue would look from any angle, how eminently suitable it was for enshrinement. But he still sat there with less expression on his face than the average C-grade servitor.

"You can see that nothing has been touched since the Insurrectionists blew the statue's head off," I said, trying to drum up his interest with a pitch. "Thus the statue has picked up yet another level of historical significance to enhance its already formidable venerability. Originally a gift from France, it has historical significance as an emblem of kinship between the American and French Revolutions. Situated as it is in the mouth of New York harbor, it became a symbol of America itself to generations of immigrants. And the damage the Insurrectionists did only serves as a reminder of how lucky we were to come through that mess as lightly as we did. Also it adds a certain melancholy atmosphere, don't you think? Emotion, intrinsic beauty, and historicity combined in one elegant piece of monumental statuary. And the asking price is a good deal less than you might suppose."

Mr. Ito seemed embarrassed when he finally spoke, "I trust you will forgive my saying so, Mr. Harris, since the emotion is engendered by the highest regard for the noble past of your great nation, but I find this particular artifact somewhat depressing."

"How so, Mr. Ito?"

The jumper completed a circle of the Statue of Liberty and began another as Mr. Ito lowered his eyes and stared at the oily waters of the bay as he answered.

"The symbolism of this broken statue is quite saddening, representing as it does a decline from your nation's past greatness. For me to enshrine such an artifact in Kyoto would be an ignoble act, an insult to the memory of your nation's greatness. It would be a statement of overweening pride."

Can you beat that? *He* was offended because he felt that displaying the statue in Japan would be insulting the United States, and therefore I was implying he was *nikulturi* by offering it to him. When all that the damned thing was to any American was one more piece of junk left over from the glory days that the Japanese, who were nuts for such rubbish, might be persuaded to pay through the nose for the dubious privilege of carting away. These Japs could drive you crazy—who else could you offend by suggesting they do something that they thought would offend you but you thought was just fine in the first place?

"I hope I haven't offended you, Mr. Ito," I blurted out. I could have bitten my tongue off the moment I said it, because it was exactly the wrong thing to say. I *had* offended him and it was only further offense to put him in a position where politeness demanded that he deny it.

"I'm sure that could not have been further from your

intention, Mr. Harris," Ito said with convincing sincerity. "A pang of sadness at the perishability of greatness, nothing more. In fact, as such, the experience might be said to be healthful to the soul. But making such an artifact a permanent part of one's surroundings would be more than I could bear."

Was this his true feeling or just smooth Japanese politeness? Who could tell what these people really felt? Sometimes I think they don't even know what they feel themselves. But at any rate, I had to show him something that would change his mood, and fast. Hmmm ...

"Tell me, Mr. Ito, are you fond of baseball?"

His eyes lit up like satellite beacons and the heavy mood evaporated in the warm, almost childish glow of his sudden smile. "Ah, yes!" he said. "I retain a box at Osaka Stadium, though I must confess I secretly retain a partiality for the Giants. How strange it is that this profound game has so declined in the country of its origin."

"Perhaps. But that fact has placed something on the market which I'm sure you'll find most congenial. Shall we go?"

"By all means," Mr. Ito said. "I find our present environs somewhat overbearing."

I floated the jumper to five hundred feet and programmed a mach 2.5 jump curve to the north that quickly put the great hunk of moldering, dirty copper far behind. It's amazing how much sickening emotion the Japanese are able to attach to almost any piece of old junk. *Our* old junk at that, as if Japan didn't have enough useless clutter of its own. But I certainly shouldn't complain about it; it makes me a pretty good living. Everyone knows the old saying about a fool and his money.

The jumper's trajectory put us at float over the confluence of the Harlem and East Rivers at a thousand feet. Without dropping any lower, I whipped the jumper northeast over the Bronx at 300 m.p.h. This area had been covered by tenements before the Insurrection, and had been thoroughly razed by firebombs, high explosives, and napalm. No one had ever found an economic reason for clearing away the miles of rubble, and now the scarred earth and ruined buildings were covered with tall grass, poison sumac, tangled scrub growth, and scattered thickets of trees which might merge to form a forest in another generation or two. Because of the crazy, jagged, overgrown topography, this land was utterly useless and no one lived here except some pathetic remnants of old hippie tribes that kept to themselves and weren't worth hunting down. Their occasional huts and patchwork tents were the only signs of human habitation in the area. This was *really* depressing territory, and I wanted to get Mr. Ito over it high and fast.

Fortunately, we didn't have far to go, and in a couple of minutes I had the jumper floating at five hundred feet over our objective, the only really intact structure in the area. Mr. Ito's stone face lit up with such boyish pleasure that I knew I had it made; I had figured right when I figured he couldn't resist something like this.

"So!" he cried in delight. "Yankee Stadium!"

The ancient ballpark had come through the Insurrection with nothing worse than some atmospheric blackening and cratering of its concrete exterior walls. Everything around it had been pretty well demolished except for a short section of old elevated subway line which still stood beside it, a soft rusty-red skeleton covered with vines and moss. The surrounding ruins were thoroughly overgrown, huge piles of rubble, truncated buildings, rusted-out tanks, forming tangled

man-made jungled foothills around the high point of
the stadium, which itself had creepers and vines growing all over it, partially blending it into the wild, overgrown landscape.

The Bureau of National Antiquities had circled the
stadium with a high, electrified, barbed-wire fence to
keep out the hippies who roamed the badlands. A lone
guard armed with a Japanese-made slicer patrolled the
fence in endless circles at fifteen feet on a one-man
skimmer. I brought the jumper down to fifty feet and
orbited the stadium five times, giving the enthralled
Ito a good, long, contemplative look at how lovely it
would look as the centerpiece of his gardens instead of
hidden away in these crummy ruins. The guard waved
to us each time our paths crossed—must be a lonely,
boring job out here with nothing but old junk and crazy
wandering hippies for company.

"May we go inside?" Ito said in absolutely reverent
tones. Man, was he hooked! He glowed like a little kid
about to inherit a candy store.

"Certainly, Mr. Ito," I said, taking the jumper out
of its circling pattern and floating it gently up over the
lip of the old ballpark, putting it on hover at roof-level
over what had once been short centerfield. Very slowly,
I brought the jumper down towards the tangle of tall
grass, shrubbery, and occasional stunted trees that covered what had once been the playing field.

It was like descending into some immense, ruined,
roofless cathedral. As we dropped, the cavernous triple-
decked grandstands—rotted wooden seats rich with
moss and fungi, great overhanging rafters concealing
flocks of chattering birds in their deep glowering shadows—rose to encircle the jumper in a weird, lost gran-
deur.

By the time we touched down, Ito seemed to be floating in his seat with rapture. "So beautiful!" he sighed. "Such a sense of history and venerability. Ah, Mr. Harris, what noble deeds were done in this Stadium in bygone days! May we set foot on this historic playing field?"

"Of course, Mr. Ito." It was beautiful. I didn't have to say a word; he was doing a better job of selling the moldy useless heap of junk to himself than I ever could.

We got out of the jumper and tramped around through the tangled vegation while scruffy pigeons wheeled overhead and the immensity of the empty stadium gave the place an illusion of mystical significance, as if it were some Greek ruin or Stonehenge, instead of just a ruined old baseball park. The grandstands seemed choked with ghosts; the echoes of great events that never were filled the deeply shadowed cavernous spaces.

Mr. Ito, it turned out, knew more about Yankee Stadium than I did, or ever wanted to. He led me around at a measured, reverent pace, boring my ass off with a kind of historical grand tour.

"Here Al Gionfriddo made his famous World Series catch of a potential home run by the great DiMaggio," he said, as we reached the high, crumbling black wall that ran around the bleachers. Faded numerals said "405." We followed this curving, overgrown wall around to the 467 sign in left centerfield. Here there were three stone markers jutting up out of the old playing field like so many tombstones, and five copper plaques on the wall behind them, so green with decay as to be illegible. They really must've taken this stuff seriously in the old days, as seriously as the Japanese take it now.

"Memorials to the great heroes of the New York Yankees," Ito said. "The legendary Ruth, Gehrig,

DiMaggio, Mantle.... Over this very spot, Mickey Mantle drove a ball into the bleachers, a feat which had been regarded as impossible for nearly half a century. Ah...."

And so on. Ito trampled all through the underbrush of the playing field and seemed to have a piece of trivia of vast historical significance to himself for almost every square foot of Yankee stadium. At this spot, Babe Ruth had achieved his sixtieth home run; here Roger Maris had finally surpassed that feat; over there Mantle had almost driven a ball over the roof of the venerable stadium. It was staggering how much of this trivia he knew and how much importance it all had in his eyes. The tour seemed to go on forever. I would've gone crazy with boredom if it wasn't so wonderfully obvious how thoroughly sold he was on the place. While Ito conducted his love affair with Yankee Stadium, I passed the time by counting yen in my head. I figured I could probably get ten million out of him, which meant that my commission would be a cool million. Thinking about that much money about to drop into my hands was enough to keep me smiling for the two hours that Ito babbled on about home runs, no-hitters, and triple-plays.

It was late afternoon by the time he had finally saturated himself and allowed me to lead him back to the jumper. I felt it was time to talk business, while he was still under the spell of the stadium and his resistance was at low ebb.

"It pleasures me greatly to observe the depths of your feeling for this beautiful and venerable stadium, Mr. Ito," I said. "I stand ready to facilitate the speedy transfer of title at your convenience."

Ito started as if suddenly roused from some pleasant dream. He cast his eyes downward and bowed almost imperceptibly.

"Alas," he said sadly, "while it would pleasure me beyond all reason to enshrine the noble Yankee Stadium upon my grounds, such a self-indulgence would only exacerbate my domestic difficulties. The parents of my wife ignorantly consider the noble sport of baseball an imported American barbarity. My wife unfortunately shares in this opinion and frequently berates me for my enthusiasm for the game. Should I purchase the Yankee Stadium, I would become a laughingstock in my own household and my life would become quite unbearable."

Can you beat that? The arrogant little son-of-a-bitch wasted two hours of my time dragging around this stupid heap of junk babbling all that garbage and driving me half-crazy, and he knew he wasn't going to buy it all the time! I felt like knocking his low-posture teeth down his unworthy throat. But I thought of all those yen I still had a fighting chance at and made the proper response: a rueful little smile of sympathy, a shared sigh of wistful regret, a murmured "Alas."

"However," Ito added brightly, "the memory of this visit is something I shall treasure always. I am deeply in your debt for granting me this experience, Mr. Harris. For this alone, the trip from Kyoto has been made more than worthwhile."

Now, that really made my day.

I was in real trouble, very close to blowing the biggest deal I've ever had a shot at. I'd shown Ito the two best items in my territory, and if he didn't find what he wanted in the Northeast there were plenty of first-rate pieces still left in the rest of the country—top stuff like the St. Louis Gateway Arch, the Disneyland Matterhorn, the Salt Lake City Mormon Tabernacle—and plenty of other brokers to collect that big fat commission.

I figured I had only one more good try before Ito
started thinking of looking elsewhere: the United Nations building complex. The U.N. had fallen into a complicated legal limbo. The United Nations had retained
title to the buildings when they moved their headquarters out of New York, but when the U.N. folded,
New York State, New York City, and the Federal Government had all laid claim to them, along with the
U.N.'s foreign creditors. The Bureau of National Antiquities didn't have clear title, but they did administer
the estate for the Federal Government. If I could palm
the damned thing off on Ito, the Bureau of National
Junk would be only too happy to take his check and
let everyone else try to pry the money out of them. And
once he moved it to Kyoto, the Japanese government
would not be about to let anyone repossess something
that one of their heavyweight citizens had shelled out
hard yen for.

So I jumped her at mach 1.7 to a hover at three
hundred feet over the greasy waters of the East River
due east of the U.N. complex at Forty-second. At this
time of day and from this angle, the U.N. buildings
presented what I hoped was a romantic Japanese-style
vista. The Secretariat was a giant glass tombstone dramatically silhouetted by the late-afternoon sun as it
loomed massively before us out of the perpetual gray
haze hanging over Manhattan; beside it, the low sweeping curve of the General Assembly gave the grouping
a balanced caligraphic outline. The total effect seemed
similar to that of one of those ancient Japanese Torii
gates rising out of the foggy sunset, only done on a far
grander scale.

The Insurrection had left the U.N. untouched—the
rebels had had some crazy attachment for it—and from
the river, you couldn't see much of the grubby open-air

market that had been allowed to spring up in the plaza, or the honky-tonk bars along First Avenue. Fortunately, the Bureau of National Antiquities made a big point of keeping the buildings themselves in good shape, figuring that the Federal Government's claim would be weakened if anyone could yell that the Bureau was letting them fall apart.

I floated her slowly in off the river, keeping at the three-hundred-foot level, and started my pitch. "Before you, Mr. Ito, are the United Nations buildings, melancholy symbol of one of the noblest dreams of man, now unfortunately empty and abandoned, a monument to the tragedy of the U.N.'s unfortunate demise."

Flashes of sunlight, reflected off the river, then onto the hundreds of windows that formed the face of the Secretariat, scintillated intermittently across the glass monolith as I set the jumper to circling the building. When we came around to the western face, the great glass façade was a curtain of orange fire.

"The Secretariat could be set in your gardens so as to catch both the sunrise and sunset, Mr. Ito," I pointed out. "It's considered one of the finest examples of Twentieth Century Utilitarian in the world, and you'll note that it's in excellent repair."

Ito said nothing. His eyes did not so much as flicker. Even the muscles of his face seemed unnaturally wooden. The jumper passed behind the Secretariat again, which eclipsed both the sun and its giant reflection; below us was the sweeping gray concrete roof of the General Assembly.

"And, of course, the historic significance of the U.N. buildings is beyond measure, if somewhat tragic—"

Abruptly, Mr. Ito interrupted, in a cold, clipped voice. "Please forgive my crudity in interjecting a political opinion into this situation, Mr. Harris, but I believe such frankness will save you much wasted time and effort and myself considerable discomfort."

All at once, he was Shiburo Ito of Ito Freight Boosters of Osaka, a mover and shaper of the economy of the most powerful nation on earth, and he was letting me know it. "I fully respect your sentimental esteem for the late United Nations, but it is a sentiment I do not share. I remind you that the United Nations was born as an alliance of the nations which humiliated Japan in a most unfortunate war, and expired as a shrill and contentious assembly of pauperized beggar-states united only in the dishonorable determination to extract international alms from more progressive, advanced, self-sustaining, and virtuous states, chief among them Japan. I must therefore regretfully point out that the sight of these buildings fills me with nothing but disgust, though they may have a certain intrinsic beauty as abstract objects."

His face had become a shiny mask and he seemed a million miles away. He had come as close to outright anger as I had ever heard one of these heavyweight Japs get; he must be really steaming inside. Damn it, how was I supposed to know that the U.N. had all those awful political meanings for him? As far as I'd ever heard, the U.N. hadn't meant anything to anyone for years, except as an idealistic, sappy idea that got taken over by Third Worlders and went broke. Just my rotten luck to run into one of the few people in the world who was still fighting that one!

"You are no doubt fatigued, Mr. Harris," Ito said coldly. "I shall trouble you no longer. It would be best to return to your office now. Should you have further objects to show me, we can arrange another appointment at some mutually convenient time."

What could I say to that? I had offended him deeply,

and besides I couldn't think of anything else to show
him. I took the jumper to five hundred and headed
downtown over the river at a slow one hundred, hoping
against hope that I'd somehow think of something to
salvage this blown million-yen deal with before we
reached my office and I lost this giant goldfish forever.

As we headed downtown, Ito stared impassively out
of the bubble at the bleak ranks of hign-rise apartment
buildings that lined the Manhattan shore below us, not
deigning to speak or take further notice of my miser-
able existence. The deep orange light streaming in
through the bubble turned his round face into a Rising
Sun, straight off the Japanese flag. It seemed appropriate. The crazy bastard was just like his country; a
politically touchy, politely arrogant economic overlord
with infinitely refined esthetic sensibilities inexplicably combined with a packrat lust for the silliest of our
old junk. One minute an Ito seemed so superior in every
way, and the next he was a stupid, childish sucker. I've
been doing business with the Japanese for years, and
I still don't really understand them. The best I can do
is guess around the edges of whatever their inner reality actually is, and hope I hit what works. And this
time out, with a million yen or more dangled in front
of me, I had guessed wrong three times and now I was
dragging my tail home with a dissatisfied customer
whose very posture seemed designed to let me know
that I was a crass, second-rate boob and that he was
one of the lords of creation!
"Mr. Harris! Mr. Harris! Over there! That magnif-
icent structure!" Ito was suddenly almost shouting; his
eyes were bright with excitement, and he was actually
smiling.
He was pointing due south along the East River.

The Manhattan bank was choked with the ugliest public housing projects imaginable, and the Brooklyn
shore was worse; one of those huge, sprawling, so-called
industrial parks, low windowless buildings, geodesic
warehouses, wharves, a few freight-booster launching
pads. Only one structure stood out, there was only one
thing Ito could've meant: the structure linking the
housing project on the Manhattan side with the industrial park on the Brooklyn shore

Mr. Ito was pointing at the Brooklyn Bridge

"The ... ah ... bridge, Mr. Ito?" I managed to say
with a straight face. As far as I knew, the Brooklyn
Bridge had only one claim to historicity: it was the butt
of a series of jokes so ancient that they weren't funny
any more. The Brooklyn Bridge was what old comic
con men traditionally sold to sucker tourists, green-
horns, or hicks they used to call them, along with phony
uranium stocks and gold-painted bricks.

So I couldn't resist the line: "You want to buy the
Brooklyn Bridge, Mr. Ito?" It was so beautiful; he had
put me through such hassles, and had finally gotten
so damned high and mighty with me, and now I was
in effect calling him an idiot to his face and he didn't
know it.

In fact, he nodded eagerly in answer like a straight
man out of some old joke and said, "I do believe so. Is
it for sale?"

I slowed the jumper to forty, brought her down to a
hundred feet, and swallowed my giggles as we approached the crumbling old monstrosity. Two massive
and squat stone towers supported the rusty cables from
which the bed of the bridge was suspended. The jumper
had made the bridge useless years ago; no one had
bothered to maintain it and no one had bothered to
tear it down. Where the big blocks of dark-gray stone

met the water, they were encrusted with putrid-looking green slime. Above the waterline, the towers were whitened with about ten years' worth of birdshit.

It was hard to believe that Ito was serious. The bridge was a filthy, decayed, reeking old monstrosity. In short, it was just what Ito deserved to be sold.

"Why, yes, Mr. Ito," I said, "I think I might be able to sell you the Brooklyn Bridge."

I put the jumper on hover about a hundred feet from one of the filthy old stone towers. Where the stones weren't caked with seagull guano, they were covered with about an inch of black soot. The roadbed was cracked and pitted and thickly paved with garbage, old shells, and more birdshit; the bridge must've been a seagull rookery for decades. I was mighty glad the jumper was airtight; the stink must've been terrific.

"Excellent!" Mr. Ito exclaimed. "Quite lovely, is it not? I am determined to be the man to purchase the Brooklyn Bridge, Mr. Harris."

"I can think of no one more worthy of that honor than your esteemed self, Mr. Ito," I said with total sincerity.

About four months after the last section of the Brooklyn Bridge was boosted to Kyoto, I received two packages from Mr. Shiburo Ito. One was a mailing envelope containing a minicassette and a holo slide; the other was a heavy package about the size of a shoebox wrapped in blue rice paper.

Feeling a lot more mellow toward the memory of Ito these days with a million of his yen in my bank account, I dropped the mini into my playback and was hardly surprised to hear his voice.

"Salutations, Mr. Harris, and once again my profoundest thanks for expediting the transfer of the

Brooklyn Bridge to my estate. It has now been permanently enshrined and affords us all much esthetic enjoyment and has enhanced the tranquility of my household immeasurably. I am enclosing a holo of the shrine for your pleasure. I have also sent you a small token of my appreciation which I hope you will take in the spirit in which it is given. Sayonara."

My curiosity aroused, I got right up and put the holo slide in my wall viewer. Before me was a heavily wooded mountain which rose into twin peaks of austere, dark-gray rock. A tall waterfall plunged gracefully down the long gorge between the two pinnacles to a shallow lake at the foot of the mountain, where it smashed onto a table of flat rock, generating perpetual billows of soft mist which turned the landscape into something straight out of a Chinese painting. Spanning the gorge between the two peaks like a spiderweb directly over the great falls, its stone towers anchored to islands of rock on the very lip of the precipice, was the Brooklyn Bridge, its ponderous bulk rendered slim and graceful by the massive scale of the landscape. The stone had been cleaned and glistened with moisture, the cables and roadbed were overgrown with lush green ivy. The holo had been taken just as the sun was setting between the towers of the bridge, outlining it in rich orange fire, turning the rising mists coppery and sparkling in brilliant sheets off the falling water.

It was very beautiful.

It was quite a while before I tore myself away from the scene, remembering Mr. Ito's other package.

Beneath the blue-paper wrappings was a single gold-painted brick. I gaped. I laughed. I looked again.

The object looked superficially like an old brick covered with gold paint. But it wasn't. It was a solid brick of soft, pure gold, a replica of the original item, perfect in every detail.

I knew that Mr. Ito was trying to tell me something, but I still can't quite make out what.

"to secure these rights..."

jerry pournelle

When I announced the second edition of this book, I asked the contributors if any of them thought events since the story had been written made their contribution unlikely or impossible. None thought so. In their judgments, these futures could happen.

Many of these futuribles are somewhat grim. Bova's economically exhausted nation; Anderson's communist America; Ellison's fascist America; Van Vogt's bureaucracy run riot; Spinrad's economic collapse; all are possible paths downhill. Unfortunately, those stories haven't exhausted the threats to civilization. Nature, we discover, isn't as friendly and benign as we'd like her to be.

For example: Out in the old Homestake mine in Montana they're searching for solar neutrinos. By every theory we have of what keeps the Sun burning, there have to be neutrinos; and we are certain that the Homestake experiment would detect them.

They haven't found any. Some theorists have suggested, not entirely whimsically, that "the Sun has gone out."

Maybe it has.

More evidence: On April 9, 1567, Christopher Clavius observed a total eclipse and described it so vividly that few doubt he saw what he says he saw. He described an "annular eclipse," one in which the rim of the Sun projects in a bright ring around the Moon. I'm told by those who've seen one that it's a glorious sight. It's also very rare, because not only must you be in the path of totality, but also the Moon has to be just far enough away; and what's disturbing is that Clavius could have seen an annular eclipse on that day only if the Sun were larger then than now.

Meanwhile, the official observatories in both the U.S. and Britain report that the Sun has shrunk by a full arc second in the last century. That's a rate of five feet an hour. It's consistent with Clavius's observations.

Has the Sun gone out? And what would that mean?

Well, what keeps the Sun large? It's only a ball of gas; if it weren't burning, it would collapse into a neutron star. However, the thermonuclear reactions inside the Sun produce vigorous photons, and those energetic light rays hold the outer layers up. If the core reactions stop, then the Sun will indeed collapse; but that collapse generates heat, and the Sun would shine on for a long time. The heat from the collapse will probably restart the fire. It's possible there have been lots of cycles like that: the Sun goes out, begins to collapse; the heat of collapse restarts thermonuclear reactions, which spread the layers out until they're too thin to support thermonuclear burning; and the cycle starts over.

These cycles would have an effect on Earth; one we ought to be able to observe.

And we do know of one such cycle in Earth's geological history. The Ice Ages are periodic, and by pure statistical projection we're due for another: for several millions of years the "normal" pattern for Earth has been Ice Ages of 100,000 years, with brief 15,000-year interruptions of warmer climate. The last full Ice Age ended about 15,000 years ago.

Meanwhile, Genevieve Woillard of the Catholic University of Louvain has been collecting samples from lake bottoms in northeastern France. The samples contain layers of pollen deposits something like tree rings, and tell with great accuracy what kind of trees—and thus what climate—prevailed in the district over the past 50,000 years.

Her experiments show that the region went from temperate forest to taiga in fewer than 150 years; and from a period of "colder winters" to glacial ice in twenty years. Other studies have shown that at the onset of the last Ice Age it took considerably fewer than one hundred years for the glaciers to cover Great Britain.

During the American Revolution, Colonel Alexander Hamilton brought cannon to General Washington on Manhattan Island by dragging them across the ice on the Hudson River. In those days the growing season was much shorter than now; and of course there's not that much ice on the Hudson even in the coldest winters. Not now.

But we had the Great Freeze of 1976-77, and the Big Freeze of 77-78, and the "severe winter" of 78-79. Are these mere flukes? Or are we due for a spate of "unusually cold winters"?

The climate experts don't know. But that's another futurible to worry about: Ice Age before the year 2000. It isn't likely; but it's possible.

And another Ice Age is inevitable if we wait long enough.

Roberto Vacca is a disturbing man. His book **The Coming Dark Age** *(Doubleday)* is a must-read for the prudent and thoughtful. I don't agree that our complex civilization must collapse; but certainly it could. Vacca points out just how dependent we are on large and com-

plex systems. Power grids interconnected, comlex distributions systems for food which are dependent on complex distribution systems for gasoline and diesel fuel; the fuel-distribution system dependent on electric power; that sort of thing. And of course no country is more than three meals from bread riots. Imagine what might happen if all the welfare and social security checks started bouncing.

This is more or less the rationale behind Spinrad's story.

Add to that the ascendancy of Suslov—sometimes known as "the last Communist"—in the Soviet Union. Add the weakness of the dollar; add our dependence on foreign oil. It's easy to feel threatened.

One major result of these threats to civilization is that a number of people have formed "survival clubs." "Survival" books and articles are increasingly popular. There's even a (very good) book called Survival Guns. *Prudent and intelligent people everywhere are making contingency plans, just in case things won't hold together.*

And that is prudent, and I have my own plans and organization, and all of us know where to go if civilization does come apart. I may feel a bit foolish holding preparedness drills, but I'd rather feel a little silly than find myself wishing ardently we had done some planning.

But that's at an individual level; and, while in a real crash there will be survivors, and those who've planned will be better off than those who haven't, the best prepared will be worse off after than before the crunch. The best survival policy is to see that the disaster doesn't happen.

Which means collective action; in a word, government. Hardly surprising to Americans. "...Among these are Life, Liberty, and the Pursuit of Happiness.

That to secure these Rights, Governments are instituted among Men . . ."

But do government's experts know what they're doing?

Not long ago I spoke at a conference. I was a preliminary event; the big attraction was a debate between Professor Arthur Laffer, a rising young economist beloved of conservatives, and Professor John Kenneth Galbraith, certainly the most distinguished and best-known economist of the liberal persuasion. Each talked for about ninety minutes. Each discussed the amazing economic growth of the sixties; in fact, the frantic sixties sounded like a Golden Age. Each contrasted the economic growth of the sixties with the stagnant seventies. Neither had a definitive theory on why the great difference.

And neither, in the entire ninety minutes, so much as mentioned the words "space," "research," "technology," "engineering," or "invention."

Yet one wonders: Was not the boom of the sixties at least in part connected to the space program; to the vigorous research and development of that decade; to high-technology engineering, with the space program the cutting edge and driving force?

By now, I expect, some readers are puzzled: Here is a book edited by Pournelle, a known space fanatic; and there isn't one story about "life in outer space." No L-5 colonies, no asteroid mines, no solar-power satellites, no space factories. A number of well-known science-fiction authors write about the realistic future, and there's very little Buck Rogers stuff. Why is this?

It puzzled me also, until I heard a talk given by Ray Bradbury.

(No, he's not in this book. I wish he were, and not

only because I very much like his work; I've also found out something peculiar about literary critics, at least those in Los Angeles, and I guess that story's worth an aside: Larry Niven and I both contributed essays to a nonfiction analysis of our art entitled The Craft of Science Fiction. *When it was reviewed in the* Los Angeles Times *we naturally thought they'd mention us local boys; but no. Instead, the review was run under a picture of Ray Bradbury, and the reviewer spent the entire column on what a shame it was that Bradbury had not written anything for the book. . . .)*

In a recent talk Bradbury pointed out something I've known for years but never thought of: that in the two most famous SF dystopias, 1984 and Brave New World, there is no space program; there are no Moon colonies or space travel. And, as Ray went on to point out, there couldn't be. Those dystopias simply couldn't happen if there were free men in space; and space tends to make freedom for its inhabitants.

And there was my explanation of this book: Most of the stories are dystopias; and it's hard to write a dystopic story if you postulate a vigorous space effort by the United States. Too many of the factors producing a dystopia vanish if you assume extensive space activities.

Which brings me back to my favorite point.

The Panama Canal was a spectacular success in an era of successes. The space program was a spectacular success in a era of spectacular failures. Both cost about five percent of the national budget for a decade. For comparable amounts we could insure the human race against most disasters; we could give the stars and planets to ourselves and our children. We could "secure the blessings of liberty for ourselves and our posterity."

We really could.